Acclaim for *My*

"Stacey Richter's comic voic
est, the most persuasive aro
which never happens, *and*
heavy metal, cybersex, Polynesian mating
stuff. Buy two copies, one for yourself and one for your aunt who infrequently smiles."

—Rick Moody, author of *The Black Veil*, *Purple America*, and *The Ice Storm*

"Stacey Richter's *My Date with Satan* is like *The Fantastic Voyage*, a sci-fi shuttle full of stories that take you inside the human body to the molten core of her characters."

—Susan Salter Reynolds, *Los Angeles Times*

"A quirky, twisted, charmingly original debut collection . . . each story delivers a flash of the Dark Side in a way that's guaranteed to make you grin."

—Cathi Hanauer, *Mademoiselle*

"*My Date with Satan* is like surfing the Web. You can never be sure who—or what—will turn up next."

—Tracy Young, *Elle*

"Really good . . . high inventiveness . . . beautifully sprawling and hallucinogenic. . . . Think Gogol, where a vanished nose sets off satire about social rank."

—Minna Proctor, *The New York Observer*

"*My Date with Satan* is filled with the kind of sexually deviant, foulmouthed tough girls who only wish Satan was as bad as the reputation that precedes him."

—Lucinda Rosenfeld, *Harper's Bazaar*

"In this collection of thirteen funny, touching tales, Richter's crackling voice reveals the hollow center of contemporary pop culture, veering seamlessly between prom night and *The Twilight Zone*."

—Jim Nintzel, *Tucson Weekly*

"The women in Richter's collection of short stories are looking for love in lots of strange places: the rat-infested apartment of the man upstairs, the seductively filthy language of the Internet geek, and a hallucinatory sexual encounter with a monster on prom night."

—Janet Steen, *US*

"The characters in Stacey Richter's collection are extremely articulate about their cluelessness. With hilarious gusto they detail but never explain the meaning behind the crises of their lives. But the locomotive insistence of their voices is what gives these stories their fierce charm."

—*The Village Voice*

"*My Date with Satan* is a great ride. . . . Richter's stories abandon niceties and drive right to the core of her characters. . . . Pure, unadulterated genius."

—Cynthia Copeland, *Pasadena Weekly*

"Richter's debut collection is daring. What's good here is really good. . . . Richter's not afraid to try anything."

—Gina Vivinetto, *St. Petersburg (Florida) Times*

"[An] intelligent, original book. The author has a definite penchant for darkly humorous situations and provides such an array of boisterous voices that a fully realized novel can't be far behind. The thirteen stories in *My Date with Satan* show a unique and budding talent hard at work."

—James Plechota, *Metrowest Daily News*

"A gasp-packed debut . . . Richter has the ability to make every urban archetype new. Her writing is bare bones, and goes straight to the bloodstream."

—Traci Vogel, *The Stranger*

"*My Date with Satan* so perfectly captures being twenty-five today that, well, I can't imagine a better description anywhere without living the age again."

—Kelly Feazelle, *The Pilot*

My Date with Satan

Stories

Stacey Richter

SCRIBNER PAPERBACK FICTION
PUBLISHED BY SIMON & SCHUSTER
NEW YORK LONDON TORONTO SYDNEY SINGAPORE

SCRIBNER PAPERBACK FICTION
Simon & Schuster, Inc.
Rockefeller Center
1230 Avenue of the Americas
New York, NY 10020

First Scribner Paperback Fiction edition 2000

Designed by Brooke Zimmer
Set in Walbaum MT
Manufactured in the United States of America

1 3 5 7 9 10 8 6 4 2

The Library of Congress has cataloged the Scribner edition as follows:
Richter, Stacey, date.
My date with Satan : stories / Stacey Richter.
p. cm.
1. United States—Social life and customs—20th century Fiction.
2. Popular culture—United States Fiction. 3. Humorous stories, American. I. Title.
PS3568.I35333M9 1999
813'.54—dc21 99-13146
CIP

ISBN 0-684-85701-4
0-684-85702-2 (Pbk)

"The Beauty Treatment" appeared in *The Mississippi Review.* "An Island of Boyfriends" appeared in *Seventeen.* "Goal 666" appeared in *Granta.* "The First Men" appeared in *Michigan Quarterly Review.* "The Ocean" appeared in *Nerve°.* "Prom Night" appeared in *LIT.* "My Date with Satan" appeared in *The Greensboro Review.* "A Prodigy of Longing" appeared in *GQ.*

ACKNOWLEDGMENTS

My thanks to Kris Dahl, James DiGiovanna, Nan Graham, Jami Macarty, Rick Moody, Brant Rumble, Richard Siken, and the editors of the magazines in which these stories first appeared, for their help, guidance, and suggestions. Thanks also to the MacDowell Colony, for the lovely cabin; and to the Arizona Commission for the Arts, for financial support.

CONTENTS

The Beauty Treatment

SHE SMILED when she saw me coming, the Bitch, she smiled and stuck her fingers in her mouth like she was plucking gum out of her dental work. Then, with a little pout, like a kiss, I saw a line of silver slide toward my face. I swear to God, I thought she'd pried off her braces. I thought she'd worked one of those bands free and was holding it up to show me how proud she was to have broken loose of what we referred to, in our charming teenage banter, as oral bondage. The next thing I know there's blood all over my J. Crew linen fitted blouse, in edelweiss—a very delicate, almost ecru shade of white, ruined now. There's blood all over the tops of my tits where they pushed out my J. Crew edelweiss linen shirt and a loose feeling around my mouth when I screamed. My first thought was Fuck, how embarrassing, then I ran into the girls' room and saw it: a red gash parted my cheek from my left temple to the corner of my lip. A steady stream of blood dripped off my jawline into the sink. One minute later, Cyndy Dashnaw found the razor blade on the concrete floor of the breezeway, right where the Bitch had dropped it.

Elizabeth Beecher and Kirsty Moseley run into the bathroom and go Oh my God, then drag me screaming hysterically, all three of us screaming hysterically, to Ms. B. Meanwhile, the Bitch slides into her Mercedes 450SL, lime green if you can believe that—the A-1 primo daddy-lac of all time—and drives off smoking Kools. I'm in the nurse's office screaming with Ms. B. calmly applying pressure and ordering Mr. Pierce, the principal, to get in gear and haul my ass to the emergency room. This is what you get from watching too much TV, I'm thinking, and believing your workaholic father when he tells you during one of his rare appearances that you're the Princess of the Universe to which none can compare. And then watching teenage girls from Detroit on *Montel*, for God's sake—the *inner city*—froth and brag about hiding razors under their tongues and cutting up some ho because she glanced sideways at the boyfriend: I mean, help me. This is the twentieth century. My father's a doctor. The Bitch's father is a developer who's covered half of Scottsdale with lifestyle condos. We consume the most expensive drugs, cosmetics, and coffee known to man. Tell me: what was she thinking?

I went to the emergency room where the nurse gave me a shot to stop the screaming and eventually my mother came down and the nurse had to give her a pill to stop her from screaming too. Once Mother had sufficiently calmed she paged Dr. Wohl, who'd done her tits, and had him run down and stitch me up with some special Indonesian silk that would make me look, he promised, like a slightly rakish movie star. Afterward, during the healing process, was when my mother really started broadcasting the wonders of Smith College and Mount Holyoke or, if worse came to worse, Mills. Women's colleges were so liberating, she said, waving her tennis elbow around to signify freedom. It was such a blessing, she said, to study without all that nasty competition and distraction from boys. That's when I knew I was in for it. If my mother, who wanted nothing more than for me to marry a Jewish doctor like she had—to duplicate her glorious life and live bored and frustrated in the suburbs and flirt with the other bald, wrinkled, fat, ugly doctors at the tennis club on Wednesday afternoons—if *this* mother was trying to usher me away from the prying eyes of young, male, pre-med students, I knew it was all over for me. I knew my looks were shot.

And another thing—as if I'd relish the thought of living with a bunch of chicks in hormonal flux after a prime example, the Bitch, my best friend, sliced a gill into my cheek for no apparent reason. Why did she do it? they kept asking. What happened between you? Ask her yourself, I replied. Ask the Bitch. But I knew she would never tell. How could she? It was bad enough that they took her down to the police station and put her in a cell without air-conditioning until her daddy showed up with *two* lawyers and escorted her out of there like she was Queen of the May Parade. It was bad enough that she got kicked out of Phoenix Country Day and had to go to Judson—*Judson,* where bad kids from California with parents who didn't want them were sent to board. At Judson, even the high school students had to wear uniforms.

Uniforms, ha ha, it served her right. After The Accident as my mother called it, or The Beauty Treatment, as my father referred to it, I was treated like that guy my verbal teacher at Princeton Review told us about, the prodigal son, but a female version. Did I shop? I shopped till I dropped. I had all the latest stuff from the stores *and* the catalogs. I had six pairs of Doc Martens, a set of sterling flatware (for my dowry), and a Chanel suit. We flew to New York to get the suit. All this accompanied by the message—through word and gesture of Arthur and Judi, doting parents—that no matter what I had, I could not have enough. Not only did I deserve this, I deserved this and more. I had suffered, and every available style of Swatch would bring relief.

The Bitch, meanwhile, was slogging through her days in a tartan skirt and knee socks. She was locked in a world without jewelry, handbags, or accessories. White shirt, button-down collar—no patterns, no decorations, no excuses. They couldn't even wear a demure white-on-white check. We got the lowdown from the Judson Cactus Wrens at soccer matches—big, bitter girls who charged the ball with clenched teeth and didn't even talk among themselves at half-time. They told us about the uniform requirements with a weird, stiff pride, like they were army recruits. Talk about future sadistic Phys Ed instructors, those Wrens were hard. Every time we had a game against them, half the Country Day girls got convenience periods and skipped out on a nurse's pass.

Even when I really did have my period, I never got a pass. I wasn't afraid of anything anymore, as long as the Bitch wasn't on the Judson soccer team, which she wasn't. I mean, what could happen that would be worse than what I had already gone through? Getting kicked in the shin? A torn earlobe? Being snubbed by Bobby English? Give me a break. I'd seen pain and passed through it. I was a superhero. I was a goddamn Jewish Joan of Arc riding a convertible Volkswagen Rabbit in a lemon yellow Chanel suit. After a few months, so many people had asked me what was wrong with my face that it stopped bothering me and I began to have fun with it. I even managed to work in some of my vocabulary words.

"I was on the back of Johnny Depp's motorcycle. He tried to feel me up, like the callow youth he is, and we wiped out."

And, "I was wearing Lee press-on nails and had the most vehement itch."

Or my personal favorite, "My father did it by accident, whilst beating me zealously," which got horrified looks, especially from medical personnel.

All in all, things weren't so bad. Everyone at school was being really nice, and I was getting extra time to make up my homework. This while the Bitch had to either go straight home from school or go directly to the shrink. Even her stupid, doting mother thought she was crazy for a day or two; I know because her mom and my mom are friends, though I must say the relationship is, oh, a bit *strained*. The Bitch must have put them off with a fake story because if she ever told the truth they'd put her in the nuthouse with her schizophrenic brother where she probably belongs. She must have told them that I had stolen her boyfriend or shafted her on a dope deal. She must have told them something that would have sounded plausible on *Oprah* or *Montel*, something gritty and real—the kind of thing they wanted. When the truth is the Bitch started hating me one day out of the clear blue after we'd been friends for six years, since we were ten years old, because I wanted to go into a store and buy the sheet music for "Brokenhearted," a song made famous by the singer Brandy.

The Bitch hated Brandy. The Bitch was going through what Mr. Nesbit, our school counselor, referred to as a *phase.* The Bitch, natural born white girl, with a special pair of Mormon panties in her dresser and her own frequent flyer miles on her own credit card, wanted to be a homegirl. She had her dishwater hair done up in scrawny braids and got paste-on acrylic nails with a charm on the ring finger that said "Nubian." She wore deep brown lipstick from the Soul Collection at Walgreen's. When her braids got frizzy, which didn't take long, she slicked them back with Afro Sheen.

I, on the other hand, did not wish to be a homegirl. I figured it was my lot to try to survive as a rich, white Jewish girl who could not do the splits and therefore would never be a cheerleader and it would be fruitless to reach for anything else. I had nothing against black people, though it's true I didn't know any. Was it my fault there weren't any black families clamoring to send their children to Phoenix Country Day? Was it my fault my parents trundled me off to a snooty private school? Hell no! I was a pawn, a child, and the worst sin I was guilty of, according to those tablets Moses obtained, was taking off my bra for Bobby English and ridiculing my loving parents whenever I got a chance. Thus, I had no longings to be a homegirl, and it pissed the Bitch off. She said I was spoiled. She said we should be tough. She said black chicks were the coolest and saw the world for what it really was—a jungle; a merciless, dog-eat-dog world.

Which struck me as strange, especially considering the Bitch had the sweetest dog in the world named, perhaps ironically, Blackie. Blackie was getting pretty old but still had some spunk. Right up to the day of the razor incident, the Bitch and I would take her out to the golf course in the evenings and let her bite streams of water shooting from the sprinklers. That dog was great. We both loved Blackie and urged her to go get the sprinklers, to really kill 'em; then she would lie down panting in the wet grass and act like she was never going to get up. The Bitch and I frequently discussed what we would do if tragedy struck and the dog died. Blackie was fourteen and had been the Bitch's companion almost her entire life. The void, the terrible void that would be left behind. We discussed filling it with taxidermy. She would have her stuffed, the Bitch said, in the sprinkler-biting posture, because that was when Blackie was the happiest, and we were the happiest sharing in her joy. She would put it on her credit card.

The loss of Blackie loomed all the more ominous, I suppose, since the Bitch's adoring father basically never came home from work and the Bitch's mother was preoccupied trying to get the schizophrenic brother either into or out of commitment. The brother was smoking a lot of pot and talking to little guys from Canada or Planet Centaur, it just depended. On occasion he'd be struck by the notion that the Bitch was the Bride of Pure Evil and one day he stuck a fork in her thigh. In return, she bit him, then took off her shirt and showed him her tits, which mortified him so much he ran around the house for a while, then curled up in the corner. After that, if he was slipping, she'd wear a nursing bra at home so she could flash him when he got out of line.

All the while Blackie padded around after the Bitch, hoping for attention. She was a nuzzler, and even if the Bitch was busy doing something else she would insinuate her nose underneath one of her hands and just freeze there, pretending to be petted. It was touching. At night she would fall into a twitchy sleep beside the Bitch's bed. Every now and then she'd struggle to her feet and go stick her nose under the Bitch's arm or foot for a minute and hold it there. It was like she had to touch the Bitch every so often to make sure she was still okay. That dog was great. In fact, Blackie was probably the one creature she could count on, aside from me, and I could see why her decrepitude made the Bitch nervous.

Around the time Blackie was fading and her brother was going insane, the Bitch started acting even more homegirl and tough and was irked to high hell that I wouldn't get with the program. She was listening to all this gangsta rap in her Mercedes and never taking off her wraparound shades until the teacher made a specific and pointed request. I mean, even our favorite teacher, Mrs. DeMarzo, who talked like Katharine Hepburn, had to tell her to take them off. She had all these garments from the mall in extra large sizes which she referred to as "dope." Of course, do I have to mention the Bitch is not one iota interested in *actually* hanging with the homegirls? I mean, she's not driving down to the South Side and having her Alpine stereo gouged from her dashboard while she rounds up some sistahs to talk jive with, or whatever. She is hanging with me and the other fair students of

Phoenix Country Day School as always, but she's acting like she's too cool for us, like she's doing us a favor.

She was annoying, but I never considered dumping her. With me, in private, she wasn't so bad. I mean, the Bitch lived right down the street and we'd been best friends since fourth grade, when being best friends really meant something. I'd only seen one miracle in my sixteen years of life and the Bitch had been its agent. The miracle wasn't much, but it was enough to make me believe that there was some kind of power floating around in the universe and that the Bitch had a little influence with it. I figured that if I stuck close to her, my life would periodically be visited by blessings and magic, like in fairy tales. What happened was this: we were eleven years old, sitting in my room on top of the rainbow Marimekko print comforter, beneath the Olympische Spiele München posters, talking animatedly and intimately about whatever. Suddenly, the Bitch gasped and pointed to the candy-colored Venetian glass chandelier my mother brought back on the trip to Europe she took without my father. A beat of time passed. And then the chandelier winked out.

Actually, the power had gone out in the whole neighborhood. If there'd been a sound or a pulse in the light, I hadn't noticed it, and when I asked the Bitch why she'd pointed at the chandelier, she said, "Because I knew something was going to happen." Oh my God, was I a bored little girl. Did I ever want to hitch my star to someone who knew something was going to happen.

So I overlooked her flaws, her erratic behavior, her insistence I smoke Kools and endure the strains of gangsta rappers calling me a bee-atch because at least around her, things were interesting. I tried to make light of her attitude, figuring it would pass, but I wasn't sacrificing anything of myself, understand? I mean, I wanted that Brandy sheet music. I didn't care that I couldn't play the piano or any other musical instrument. That wasn't the point. I wanted "Brokenhearted" because it had this great picture of Brandy, a beautiful girl, on the cover and I thought it was cool. Me, *I* thought it was cool. Well, the Bitch was just not having any of this. For one thing, Brandy's black, which apparently is her territory and she's the big fucking expert. For another thing, she says Brandy is "an ugly little crossover wimp" and not a real homegirl and I'm an asshole if I like her. I mean, so what? So, I like Brandy. So shoot me. So pitch a fit, which she did, peeling out in her 450SL and leaving me in the parking lot of a C-mall. So slice my face with a fucking razor blade.

Which she did the next time I saw her and I haven't seen her since, except for that one time at her shrink's office. This was after my mother had gotten all high and mighty because I'd only scored 590 on the quantitative part of the SAT, since math was right after lunch and frequently, I attended stoned. Of course, Judi couldn't give a shit if I did math or not; she hires an accountant to balance her checkbook, but since my youthful beauty was trampled she'd reasoned that I should fall back on my next best asset—the mind. Oh those smart girls! Do men ever love those clever girls! She said it over and over, with a fake, bright smile, when she thought I wasn't paying close attention.

I wasn't half as worried about my sullied good looks as she was. Doctor Wohl said we could smooth out the lumps with dermabrasion, plus he wasn't entirely wrong about the rakish charm. I'd begun wearing black Anna Sui numbers and hanging out at The Coffee Plantation in Biltmore Fashion Square, where the neo-beatnik kids considered me sort of a god. I rarely spoke and they were under the impression I had a boyfriend in France. I'd also realized the scar sort of went with the curves of my face, it cupped my cheekbone—I mean, if you're going to have a major facial scar, this was the one to have. One girl with piercings all over her nose came up to me and asked where I had it done.

It wasn't like I looked normal, but I was learning to adjust. I was feeling okay about myself—I rented *The Big Heat*, where the heroine gets coffee flung in her face, and I was beginning to feel like being maimed was kind of romantic. I mean, I got noticed, and I looked just fine from the right side. Still, Judi was putting all bets on the intellect and had dragged Arthur into her camp. Together they forced me to take a Princeton Review class to get my test scores up. I hated it all except vocabulary: *Perfidy:* betrayal, the deliberate breaking of trust. *Refractory:* resisting treatment, unmanageable. My verbal was 780. 780—that's almost perfect! I couldn't believe they were making me. It had been years since they'd forced me to do anything. It was cutting into my spare time, and it wasn't only me who suffered: I knew the neo-beatniks would be lost without their tragic center. Finally I went on strike and refused to eat in the dining room. I just took a plate, retired to my room, locked the door, and put on my headphones. A couple days of this, I thought, and they'll go into serious parenting withdrawal.

The second day Mom caved and weaseled her way in. She said I could quit the class if I'd do something for her. She said she'd talked to the Bitch's mother, and she'd said her therapist had recommended I go to one of the Bitch's sessions. She "wasn't happy," Judi said; she was "having trouble adjusting." This was like one of those moments when my mother gets all doe-eyed and yearns to save the environment, but a second later it's *snap!* time for a manicure. But she was dead serious, and I knew this was my chance to get out of that fucking class. Even so, I wouldn't have done it. I wasn't scared of anything then except the Bitch. I thought I saw her a million times, in the mall or the cineplex; I saw her big, smiling head gliding through the crowd, and then a swish of silver. At the last minute it was never her—the big head always morphed into some alternate head—but whether I created it or not, I felt like I was being stalked. Then I had these dreams where the Bitch and I were just hanging out, dancing to Chaka Khan, just hanging out like before when everything was normal—and those really gave me the creeps. I did not want to see her. No Bitch for me.

But then I changed my mind. Young and foolish I am. Also, I loved the idea of going to see the Bitch's shrink. I pictured a distinguished man with gray at his temples gasping at the sight of my scar when I walked in the room. Then, he would look at me with infinite compassion. I would take a seat on the leather lounger. My outfit is DKNY. My shoes are Kenneth Cole. The Bitch would be sitting in a straight-backed chair, her hair in cornrows. The Doctor would shake his head reproachfully.

"I never dreamed the wound was so dramatic," he says.

The Bitch would blush. I notice her body racked by waves of contrition. In her arms is an album by Brandy. A CD would be more practical but I like the way an album fills up her arms.

"This is for you," she'd say. "I've learned that it's okay for us to like different things. I celebrate your appreciation of Brandy."

I thank her. The Doctor looks on approvingly. I can tell by his glance that he thinks I'm a brave and noble girl. A few minutes later I leave. The Bitch is weeping softly. I feel a light, crisp sense of forgiveness. The Doctor has offered me free therapy, if I should ever want to share my burdens.

Well I'm here to tell you, buddy, it wasn't like that at all. First, there's no lounger, and the doctor is a streaked blond chick about my mother's age. I arrive late and she shows me to the office where the Bitch is already sitting on a swivel chair. She barely looks up when I enter the room. My dress is DKNY. The Bitch is dressed like white trash in jeans and a T-shirt of normal proportions. She looks like hell. I mean, *I* look better than she does. I was always prettier than she was but she used to seem intriguing. Before, if she was in a room, you felt her presence immediately. The girl knew how to occupy space. Something came out of her—a lot of pesky teen rage but at times, something nicer. She had that glow, at least to me; she had a sense of excitement and wonder. But in the office she seems dulled, and the truth is, right away I feel sorry for the Bitch.

The Shrink looks like she came straight out of a Smith alumnae magazine—Ann Taylor suit, minimal makeup, low-heeled leather shoes. The picture of emotional efficiency. Her office, too, is a symphony in earth tones. She checks me and the Bitch out, then says something like, "Katie's been grappling with the conflict that occurred between the two of you, and now she needs to know how you feel about it."

She does not blink twice at my scar. She does not look at me with infinite compassion. I realize whose turf I'm on. She's an employee, and the Bitch's father writes the paychecks.

"I feel okay," I say. I keep trying not to look at the Bitch, but she's unavoidable. After hallucinating her face a million times, it's unnerving how unfamiliar she seems. She's gained weight, but it seems like she's not really there. There's something inert and lumpen about her. No rage, no nail charms. Nothing extreme. She's just examining her shoes—for God's sake—clogs.

"Just okay? Because Katie and I have been discussing the impact of the cutting, and for her it's really been quite profound."

The Bitch does not say anything. The Bitch is not looking at me. The Bitch is sitting with her head down and her mouth closed like the first day she came to school with braces. Then I realize something. "She's not even looking at it," I say. "She won't even check out the scar!"

I look at the Shrink like she's some kind of referee. She, apparently, is having none of that, and sits quite calmly glancing at the Bitch and me as though we were a light piece of entertainment intended to gaily pass the time. This goes on for a while. The Bitch looks at her clogs and a brown spot on the carpet. I look at the Bitch for as long as I can, then start reading the spines of the Shrink's books. *Personality Disorders*—ha, that should come in handy. I can hear the Bitch breathing, which is odd, because in all the years we hung out together I never noticed her breathing. It's like she's alive in some weird, biological way—the way those pithed frogs were alive in science class. Alive but damaged.

Finally, the Bitch clears her throat. She raises her head until her eyes hit the scar. She starts to wince, then freezes. I can tell she's trying to control her expression, but all the color drains out of her face in a smooth, descending line, like she's been pumped full of pink fluid and someone has pulled the plug.

That was when I knew for sure that I looked like shit, absolutely and for certain. I'd been fooling myself, believing I looked dashing and rascally, but in the shock on my best friend's face I saw the truth. I was ruined.

The Bitch started to cry. I started to cry. The Shrink tried to glance calmly at us as if we were a light piece of entertainment but you could sense the strain. I pulled a Kool out of my bag and lit it. The Shrink finally cracked and shot me a dirty look but I was beyond caring. I realized, after all I'd been through, that I still smoked Kools, just like the Bitch always had, like she'd encouraged me to, and the thought of that made me cry even harder. Something switched then and I wasn't crying about my face anymore. I was crying because the Bitch was the Bitch, and the friend I'd had since I was a kid, the friend who knew for certain something was going to happen to us, something magical and vivid, was lost forever. She was lost to us both. The wonder had been extinguished.

Eventually I got ahold of myself and squashed the Kool out in a piece of damp Kleenex. The Bitch had slumped over in her swivel chair and I didn't even want to look at her. My thoughts: fuck, shit, etc. It was weird. I began to feel practically like she was my friend again, us having had a simultaneous cry. I did not want that. I wanted her to stay the Bitch.

"Oh God," she says, unprompted by the Shrink.

I notice her braces are off. She's not looking at me. It's too much for her.

"Fuck," she says, to a spot on the carpet, "I'm really sorry."

Okay: I'm a girl who's going to Smith College. I'm going to Smith and then I'm going to law school to become a criminal lawyer who champions the rights of the victimized and oppressed. I'm going to have two cars, a Volvo for transportation and a Jag for thrills. I'll cut a feline figure in my Agnès B. clothes and I'll have a drawerful of jewels. Maybe I'll even get married to some average-looking dork, but I will never be pretty and I will never be loved by the handsome men who roam this earth. My dear mother told me long ago that youth and beauty will get you everything. Well, mine's fucked up and now I'll never have Everything. No magic, no wonder, no fairy tales.

My plan was to walk out of there with a light, crisp sense of forgiveness, but help me. I sat in a sea of beige and looked at the Bitch in her clogs, fat, miserable, and afraid, and I knew: if I really forgave her, something vast and infinite would open up inside me, some place wide and blue, and I couldn't enter such a place. It would be like some kind of health spa—where you go in naked, without any things. God, would I ever be lost in a place like that.

So I said, Oh Katie, that's okay, babe! No problema! I forgive you! with a hint of fake innocence in my voice—a little dose of manufactured niceness. She turned white again and the Shrink started urging me to get in touch with my feelings but you know, I had my finger right on them.

Later, when I got home, I went into the bathroom and stared at myself in the mirror for a while. It was the same mirror Katie and I used to stare at in the pitch black while chanting "Bloody Mary, Bloody Mary" over and over until we hallucinated the beheaded head of Mary Queen of Scots emerging in reflection, dripping like a porter-house steak. She fought her way up from the land of the dead to punish us for tempting the dark with the sight of her terrible wound. Mary with her disgusting necklace of blood—she was a perfidious one! I didn't look anything like her. In fact, I had a certain glow about me. I was so radiant I looked almost pretty. From the right side, I actually was pretty.

An Island of Boyfriends

SOMETIMES I feel like the punch line to a *Cathy* cartoon: a pair of stumpy arms flap by my sides and the balloon says, "How far does a girl have to go to meet a nice guy!!?" My plan was just to go to New Zealand. I wasn't going to meet guys, I was just going. I didn't exactly flunk out of college anyway. I was getting bad grades, and then I took a hiatus to wait tables for a while. It's hard to figure out what to do with your life, especially when you're surrounded by lowlifes. My dad said he'd pay for the summer anthropology cruise since it was educational, and I'd get to travel with a variety of college students who probably weren't addicts. This is the kind of thing I would have argued with before, but after my boyfriend Cain went into detox I got tired of arguing. I just wanted out.

And then, and then, and then. Well, I'm truly sorry everybody else on the boat drowned. I really am. I'm even sorry about Evan Fontenblue, who was just using me to make his ex-girlfriend jealous. I don't know, maybe they didn't drown. It was night, it was stormy, there was a huge thunk and the next thing I knew I was thrashing in the chilly waters of the Pacific. Maybe they all got picked up by a cruise ship. Maybe they ate lobster on deck and then got dropped off in Australia and Evan and his ex went for an amusing surf. *I* was plunged into water as dark as ink, choking on rain, struggling to keep my head up. I couldn't even tell which way up was. I had a swimming instructor when I was five who would open his arms and croon "swim to me," and I'd labor toward him, but he kept backing up and backing up, so I had to struggle farther than I could really swim, and I was coughing and drowning and almost dying. I hated that asshole! And it was just like that after the boat sank: *swim to me, swim to me*—I could hear something in the night murmuring this. And I kept swimming and swimming but there was nothing there. No arms to swim into. No bottom to touch.

I guess I'm lucky, because after a while I knocked my nose on a piece of wood. I hauled myself onto it, shaking from the cold, and silently thanked Diego, my fascist trainer, for all the pull-ups and bench presses he'd put me through. I thought those muscles were for decoration only, but they came in handy for once that night.

When the sun rose, the storm had cleared and I found myself drifting toward a green finger of land. I kicked a little, but the current pretty much sucked me up and spat me out on a beach, the kind of beach you see in a brochure for getting away from it all: wedding white sand crusted with conch shells, turquoise water fringed with tiny breakers. I crawled up on the sand and prayed for a pair of sunglasses to wash up beside me, it was all so blinding and beautiful. At the edge of the beach was a thick curtain of greenery. The only plants I recognized were palms.

I had nothing at all. I was wearing the tank top and undies I slept in. I used to get tons, literally *tons,* of mail-order catalogs from every single maker of women's apparel in the English-speaking world. I had this routine where I had to go through all of them, it was like a game: la, la la, what if I *had* to buy an outfit from this catalog? What if I was stranded on an island and this was my only source for obtaining clothing? Would I stoop to wearing that secretary-style pantsuit with slimming princess seams? I was finally on that island, only without catalogs.

No phone, no lights, no motor cars. I knew, from the classes I'd been taking on the ship, that most locations that could sustain human life, even tiny atolls ankle deep in guano, did sustain human life. Homo sapiens were determined to cram themselves into every available niche. If there were only seabirds and fresh water available someplace, humans would be there, stalking seabirds and guzzling water, probably making some sort of sacramental beer from feathers and dew. This island looked bigger, lusher, and wetter than a coral atoll. It was big enough that I couldn't even tell how big it was. But I couldn't find anyone. I looked for power lines. At night I scanned for lights. I wandered the beach in my tank top and panties, searching for footprints in the sand. When I eventually found them, they were my own.

I loitered on the beach for days, obeying the rule that says to stay in one place if you're lost. I drank rainwater puddled in the rocks. For food I just ate whatever looked like something you'd get at a really authentic sushi bar:

shellfish and urchins and dark green seaweed. I craved soy sauce. I slept in a heap of warm sand, but by dawn I was shivering. Thank God for tropical weather, or I would have frozen stiff.

I was quite the little survivalist, but after a few days I thought I was losing my mind. There was just nothing, nothing all around me, and my mind kept going: *Water, water everywhere and not a drop to drink.* I was getting too much sun. Then my mind started to go: *I want to be a part of it, New York, New York.* It was like being in some Club Med sensory deprivation chamber. Of all the different native customs I'd learned about, I hadn't heard of any where people lived alone, without any other people, unless they're on some sort of vision quest, where basically they're trying to freak themselves out for a specific religious purpose. Never in my life had I had a specific religious purpose, but I was freaking myself out anyway.

Then my fresh water dried up. As I squatted on the beach, licking a damp rock, it dawned on me that I would have to go into the jungle, even though I didn't feel like it. It was dark and snaky in there. All the plants were laced together so tightly that I would have to hack through, but I didn't have anything to hack with. So, I don't know, I just went. I had no choice, and I was feeling weird, like I had PMS, but deeper. I crawled through those fucking vines on my hands and knees for hours at a stretch. I shimmied up tree trunks and tried to swing over the undergrowth, Jane-style. I didn't find any water for the first few days. I didn't know what plants were eatable, so I just gnawed on anything that looked vaguely fruity. My mind kept going: *If I can make it there, I'll make it anywhere.* But I wasn't sure I was going to make it.

And on and on. I don't know exactly what happened after a point. I was alone, and I was hungry and thirsty and bitchy and my legs itched where the hair was growing in. I crawled around the jungle for weeks, sucking on fruit and birds' eggs, lapping water from seeps, but nothing seemed right. I couldn't locate a good supply of clear, running water. I kept hallucinating soda machines. The jungle canopy made me claustrophobic, and it rained bird shit on me all day. I took it personally.

When I saw the first boyfriend, I was giddy with relief. I'd pretty much resigned myself to wandering alone in the jungle for the rest of my life, when this tall, good-looking tribal guy stepped out of a background of green, wearing a stitched loincloth made of hide, with smears of charcoal snaking across his chest. I was scared I guess, but mostly I thought, Thank God. Another person. He actually looked cool, you know, he had flair. Something about his face reminded me of Tom Cruise, even though he had darker skin and a headdress of white shells and a tattoo on his cheek; and he was carrying a bow and arrow and spoke in some guttural-whistling language I still haven't been able to catch on to, very well. He approached me slowly and made a dip, a sort of curtsy. I made one back and he laughed. Nice teeth. I thought: Okay! I can do this.

He seemed really, really happy to see me. Right away he gave me some water and a rope of dried meat. He solemnly lifted off his headdress and arranged it on my head. Then he stroked my forehead, firmly, and smiled at me in this wide and goofy way that seemed so completely overjoyed. Even then, at first contact, I was worried he might think we were married. I guess I was already feeling cagey about commitment with Tom.

He led me back to the camp. There was a whole tribe of guys there, living in huts in a clearing. I gotta say, they were all really cute. In the past, when I'd met guys from other cultures or whatever, they just looked wrong. European guys don't bathe, wear embarrassing bikini underwear, and seem sort of gay; Canadian guys bathe all the time and look really, really gay. But these guys seemed totally normal. They bathed the right amount, their hair was cool, and their loincloths weren't too small or too big. I don't know, obviously I was lonely and disoriented, but it looked to me like someone had kidnapped an assortment of hot boys from hip nightclubs in New York or LA, smuggled them to the island, and decked them in animal skins.

Boy, were they surprised to see me. I think these guys were undiscovered, as in, they'd never had contact with the outside world. They were like those Stone Age tribes they found in the highlands of Papua New Guinea in the 1930s who had no idea that people in the rest of the world knew how to use napkins and fly big metal objects through the air. The boyfriends were like that—just totally into their own thing. They hunted and made tools from stone and bone chips, and on the side they did a little cultivating of yams, a little scavenging and gathering. When they weren't occupied with those activities, they played games or music.

I'm probably not the best person to be an observer of this tribe. I feel sorry for the outside world, especially for the anthropology professors on the boat who would have given a kidney for a chance to observe an undiscovered people, with customs unadulterated by Christianity and TV and radios. These guys have a purity to them, at least they did before I came along. For a while, living in the jungle, I kept getting the Froot Loops jingle stuck in my head: *Follow your nose / It really knows! / The flavor of fruit / Wherever it grows!* I'd see a toucan and pow, there it was. But these guys don't have that. Their minds are unpolluted by jingles or pop music of any kind. No one's face reminds them of a celebrity. To them, nothing tastes like chicken.

The point is, I have sometimes wished that I was not so special to these guys. When gold prospectors first entered the New Guinea Highlands, the natives thought they were ancestral spirits who had returned to dance with them. To a lesser extent, the boyfriends seemed to think something similar of me. When I entered their camp, they pressed around me from all sides. All of them, about twenty-five guys, started clucking and whistling at once, like they were trying to coax a dog out from under a bed. A pair stepped forward to finger my hair, and one poked my boobs. Tom held my hand tightly and smiled, but his hand was slick with sweat. One by one, the boys said something, probably their names. I had no idea what they were saying. It was like they were coughing. But I felt their friendliness. I could tell they were glad I had shown up. I had a feeling they'd been waiting for me.

There weren't any women on the island, and there still aren't any except me. I don't know where they got off to. I don't know if they died from a disease or paddled away in canoes. Obviously the boyfriends didn't appear out of thin air. But I haven't had much luck with asking, and they haven't exactly volunteered an explanation. Maybe there's a tribe of girlfriends camped on a neighboring island. Maybe they're hanging out, weaving baskets, waiting around for the boys to discover them and start messing up their lives.

Tom took me to his hut. It was set apart from the others, so it might have been a special hut that had been prepared for my arrival. In case a girl showed up. What can I say about Tom? He was very sweet; a really, really nice guy. And I loved that hut. It was tidy and decorated with flowers and plaits of bright feathers. Sunlight poured through the open sides, but the thatching kept us warm and dry. Tom treated me like a princess. He prepared food and brought me water in some kind of animal bladder. He chewed hides in the evening until they were buttery, murmuring words I couldn't understand but which seemed kind. With the hides he fashioned me a lovely tunic that looked sort of like a Diane Von Furstenburg wrap dress. He escorted me on walks around the area, showing me streams and secret waterfalls and groves of fruit growing nearby. In the evening, he'd rub oil into my feet while I ate tiny birds he'd roasted over the fire. He gave me things I wanted before I even knew I wanted them, so attentive was he, so attuned. I'd often find flower petals scattered across my sleeping pallet.

We became lovers. In bed, he was tender and attentive and sweet—almost unsure of himself, but then, not. When we got right down to it, he definitely knew what to do, I can tell you that. Maybe this was one of those tribes where the older women schooled adolescent boys in the art of lovemaking. If once there had been some older women around. But by then it was just me; me and Tom, and I could tell he was hoping to keep me away from the rest of the boys. He wasn't mean about it, or obvious, but whenever we joined the others to play games or listen to music, or eat a big mammal they'd slaughtered, Tom stayed glued to my side. He held my hand constantly. If I started to talk—okay, not talk—but interact with another boy, Tom's handsome face drooped sadly, like I had just ripped his heart out of his chest, rolled it in the dirt, and danced on it.

You just can't clutch. Clutching doesn't work. I had a sense that Tom wanted to love and tend to me forever. It was like living in a hole. We started to bicker. He would cook me elaborate meals, and sometimes I'd take a tiny bite and spit it out onto the ground, just to hurt his feelings.

One warm and balmy night, I fell for another guy. He was sitting on a stump playing a wooden, stringed instrument, and he was wicked good at it. I called him Axel, just for the hell of it. I mean, there was no way I could pronounce his real name. He called me something like Shalumph. They all called me Shalumph. By then, Tom had made me a lot of clothes, and I remember I was flouncing around in a tiny halter dress that looked like something one of the girls wore in *The Flintstones.* All the boyfriends were gathered around a high, smoky bonfire while their shadows jumped and lashed at the ground. Some were drumming or playing wooden flutes, others were dancing in circles or just kicking back, grooving to the music. I hunkered on a rock beside Tom, who had his arm draped over my shoulder. I couldn't take my eyes off Axel. His long, shiny hair fell just to the top of his nipples. He had dark eyes crowned by a monobrow. When his eyes met mine, my insides liquefied. I went to him that night in his hut, and never went back to Tom's, except once, to pick up the clothes he'd made for me.

I was very happy with Axel. His hut wasn't as kempt as

Tom's, so I fixed it up a little—swept and garlanded it with flowers and stuff. Axel didn't seem to mind, and I was glad to finally have something to do. He could only cook this one weird egg stew with roots, so cooking became my department. I didn't mind, or I might have minded sometimes, but Axel was so damned sexy I forgave him. I'd become stupid with lust just watching the way he moved, how he would reach for objects in our hut with his long arms without getting up. I was fascinated by the way blossoms and feathers clung to his body hair. Every time he played his stringed instrument, I fell in love with him all over again. This was even more powerful if there were other guys around watching. Because then I could see he was so much better than they were.

We had problems, though. Axel could be a honey, but he was jealous. If he caught me dropping my gaze to another boy's loincloth, he'd drag me off into the jungle, without a word, like I was his dog. For a while I figured okay, he's a caveman, and I stayed around the hut as much as I could to reduce friction. But I got sick of it. Especially if I said anything to Tom, Axel would freak out. (Tom continued to be very sweet to me, though the baby-seal-about-to-be-clubbed look got old.)

Then Axel starting drinking the fermented beverage the tribe made out of tree sap, and hitting it hard. I can't count how many times he came back to the hut, close to dawn, drunk, with his teeth stained green from gnawing hallucinogenic bark. He'd stomp inside, peeved and disoriented, and start demolishing our things. He'd knock over a bouquet of flowers and grind my clothes in the dust, his hair all matted from crawling through the undergrowth. The worst thing he ever did, besides hit me, was to pee into the hearth. I mean, you just don't pee in your own hearth. He would say things to me then—I didn't understand what he was saying exactly, but from the way he said it, with greenish teeth and a wild halo of leaves poking out of his hair, I knew he was being really mean. Then he would expect me to give him a blow job.

I tried everything. I tried talking, gesturing, and refusing relations. He was a drunk, you know, I wanted him to stop drinking. I wanted it really badly. But when I think back on those days now, they have a charming nostalgia for me; it was like there was some kind of rope binding me to Axel then. I guess I was into the mystique of the bad boy. I'd watch his hair fall across his face, while shafts of light stabbed through the walls of the hut, and my stomach would tumble over itself with desire. I'd want him so badly I'd have to sit down and breathe through my mouth. He seemed so distant and dangerous and different from me.

I think I liked wanting something. I found it fascinating. I'd obsess about Axel's drinking problem all day, consumed with wanting: wanting him to give it up, wanting him to be peachy to me, wanting him to stop polluting our hearth and slapping me when he was in a bad mood. I'd walk around the jungle singing: *Stop, in the name of love.*

I tried being a good girl, I tried threats, and I tried that old reliable, the silent treatment. I kept asking him to stop, with my pathetic little vocabulary, until one day he actually did. When he knew I was really serious, when things between us had become so strained that I wouldn't even groom nits off his back anymore, he swore off the sap altogether. He did it for me, I could tell, and he did it without pouting. In the evenings, when a bunch of the other boys were out partying, he would turn to me with a generous smile and kiss me softly on the nose. Then we'd stroll home together. We began to spend peaceful nights in the warm dome of our hut. He played his instrument for me, and I made stews for him, and when we were done, he helped me clean the dishes.

Not long afterward, I became infatuated with a boyfriend I called Diego, after my trainer back in the States. Diego had great big arms, and I was into that. Diego was good with a spear, but he was vain. He was fastidious about his body adornments, and sometimes when we met out in the jungle to fool around, I could tell from the way he held his chest that he was trying to keep me from smearing his charcoal body markings. That made me paranoid that he might be gay, or bisexual. If I really *was* an anthropologist, I probably would have been more attentive to sexual practices among tribal members. If all of those boys were so willing to be boyfriends to me, maybe they were also willing to be boyfriends to each other? The thought made me crazy; just the idea of Diego doing it with another boyfriend gave me acne.

Diego and I tried to hide our affair from Axel, but you know how boys talk. When Axel found out, he delivered an ultimatum: no more Diego or I would be cast out of his wonderful hut. He communicated this to me with stick figures drawn in the dust, mainly a picture of a crumpled Shalumph weeping after she was cruelly separated from her adored Axel.

Well, that's not how it went. I *did* move out, and moved in with Diego for a while, but by then I wanted my own hut. Tom offered to help me build one. Actually, he built it for me, and it was just adorable—round, with a thatch-covered porch and a flap of hide for a door. I began to enjoy my freedom. There were a lot of guys in the tribe, a lot of boyfriends. I took advantage of it. I felt like I had a bumper sticker plastered to my ass: *So many men, so little time.*

Some old-fashioned sense of morality led me to stick with serial monogamy for a while. One by one, I went through a dozen of the boyfriends, looking for chemistry. I'd find it briefly before it would dissolve. Then I thought *whatever*, and started sleeping around with a vengeance. I'd have sex with one guy after lunch and another at night. I was totally open about it. I played one boyfriend off against the other, letting them know they'd have to compete in acts of strength or bravery if they wanted to bed me. Boyfriends wrestled for my favors. They butted heads and heaved spears. When that was no longer satisfying, I tried getting kinky. I cajoled two boys into having sex with me at once. I got three wasted on sap and had sex with them, too. Sometimes I heard the boyfriends around the camp muttering "Shalumph," in a bitter tone, and I wondered if it meant "princess" or "slut." I wanted it to mean both. There was something, some elusive morsel I was trying to get out of the boyfriends, but no matter how elaborately I fucked them, it never felt like I had it. I kept trying anyway. After a while, I stopped making up names for them. I called them all *boy*.

On the anthropology cruise we studied matrilineal cultures, some polygynous and patrilineal ones, but I can't remember ever hearing of another culture where one, lone girl has an endless supply of willing boyfriends. If there are others, I'd be interested to learn if the girls in them are like me. Would any woman, given the chance, keep bouncing from boyfriend to boyfriend for all of her days? It seems logical, given the habit of Homo sapiens to occupy every single available niche. There are twenty-five different boyfriends for me here; there are hundreds of different ways for me to be a girlfriend. Why wouldn't I want to sample them all?

The strange part is I got sick of it. It was like I was living in Eden, and all I could dream of was being cast out. It was too easy and smooth, and the boyfriends were so accommodating and honest. If they were fucked up or broken in some way, then they were willing to let me fix them; and if there was something I didn't like about one, he was eager to make a change. Whatever I did, no matter how much of a brat I was, those guys forgave me. There was never any room to want anything. It was like the opposite of the swimming lessons I took when I was five. Wherever I turned, someone was whispering "swim to me." Wherever I went, I fell into another boy's arms.

So I built a hut on an outcropping about a mile from the tribal village. I constructed it myself, so it sags a little, and termites have been snacking on the floor, but it's mine. It's very pleasant up here. I have a view of the jungle, and when the wind shifts, I can smell the sea. I spend the days by myself, doing regular tasks—chipping out arrowheads or grinding seeds. I feel clearer; my thoughts aren't so crowded by pop songs anymore, though lately a piece of a lonely one has been lilting through my head: *I was dancing with my darlin' to the Tennessee Waltz. . . .* Then it drifts away. Then it repeats.

Sometimes I go down and hang out with the guys on feast days, but I get nervous when they try to touch me.

Most of the time I am I guess what you'd call a hermit. I'm trying to discover something, I suppose, for personal or religious reasons, weird as that sounds. I think living on an island of boyfriends has changed me. I'm more introspective—I'd like to discover what I want or who I am, something along those lines. I want to find out why none of the boyfriends, or combination of boyfriends, has ever seemed right. The boys have been extremely accommodating. They've indicated that I should take as much time as I want; as long as I need. Whenever I'm ready, they'll be there waiting for me. And if I'm never ready, that's okay too.

Sometimes lately, I find myself wishing a real anthropologist would discover the island and study us. He could write up a description of the tribe of boyfriends, with just the one girlfriend cloistered above them in the cliffs, and analyze how the customs of the society have adapted to this unusual situation. Maybe the anthropologist could learn the language, and have a little powwow with the boys to get an idea of what they think of life here, because I have no idea. He could do an interview of me too and include that, along with some detailed analysis that would tell students back in the States how to understand my role. That's one paper I'd like to get my hands on. Maybe it would say if I was happy here or not.

Goal 666

WE MUST love nature, and we must rape nature for Satan! What would daylight be without the night? What would a clearing be without the woods? All your fairy dust, all your little white Christmas lights that twinkle, your Stardust Woman on the lite rock radio station—it would all be nothing without the dark and heavy elements of Doom/Black Metal music. When I'm onstage I feel aggression, power, rage—the everlasting lust for domination! The other side is the feminine side, the soft and pink parts that must also be cherished, as the moon is cherished, but we must remember this: we are not of the light. We are the harbingers. We are Lords of Sludge, the most revered Doom/Classical Goth Metal band in Washington State!

The Vikings did nothing but invade! Those fur-covered Goths were crazy and ultimate, the baddest of ass. When a Viking died he went to Valhalla, an indoor heaven where dead warriors engaged in perpetual battle!

The northern tradition continues still, with hellish great Scandinavian metal bands like Dissection, Dark Tranquillity, Exhumation, and Wizards of Ooze playing some of the most malevolent tunes to which Lord Satan ever lifted a pointed ear! I have the deepest reverence for the Norderland tradition, which was why I was honored to join Lords of Sludge, a Swedish heavy metal band that lost their lead singer when he ran off to become a hermit. He's practicing asceticism in the deepest forest! Their loss, my gain—since I'd been perfecting my top-secret method of Satanic throat singing and was finally ready to be a part of a great Doom/Black Metal band like Lords of Sludge. I'd been known as a tenor in church choir, but by wedging a ping-pong ball behind my teeth I perfected a means of producing a low rumble in the back of my throat that was evil in the extreme. Black Metal is spirit and power!

The three Swedish lads came from the cold land town of Uppsala, and were covered with tattoos of screaming skulls and flaming crosses—pussying great! That was my first impression. Like their Viking ancestors they were ultra-pale with fierce hanks of hair falling in dirty curtains around their faces. I thought, These are manly men! and after the audition we all slapped each other on the backs and had a hearty laugh over the throbbing music—punctuated by light, lilting passages of classical acoustic guitar—that we would produce for the Dark Lord, who was a die-hard metal fan as every die-hard metal fan knows. Those crazy Swedes! That first night they introduced me to the tradition of the sauna, which they'd built of stone and wood in the back of the house they'd rented and painted entirely black, inside and out. After we were sufficiently heated, Anders, the lead guitarist, a strapping Swedish man with mega-antisocial facial tattoos and a wide, hairless chest, led us naked and sweating into the lush, snowy woods beyond the house. We rolled our bare, hot bodies in the fresh winter snow—ah nature, we must love nature and rape it for Satan—we leapt around like satyrs scouring the woods for wayward virgins. Men! We were naked men, three Swedish and one American.

After that night we had a masculine bond, so I was slow to notice details I might have caught earlier. Though Anders had mega-fierce tattoos and Stefan, the small but muscular drummer, had huge, furry sideburns creeping across his cheeks, and Max had the extremely satanic name of Max—there was something not right about these men. There was an air of innocence to them. Despite the fiery badness of The Lords, and their lusty embrace of songs I had written, these guys were scrupulous about washing their hands after using the bathroom. They returned all their phone calls promptly and refrained from resting their forearms on the dinner table. Going for a meal with these guys was like going to a tea party: napkin on the lap, chewing with the mouth closed, salad fork, dessert spoon, and so on.

The contagion was severe. Before I knew it I was uttering phrases like, "Would you mind turning up the treble in my monitor just a smidgen?" Our leader, Anders, would bound into practice, right on time, his strong Nordic features aglow, so filled with vitality that the little spiral tattoo on his cheek seemed to twirl. Ten minutes later, the two of us were deep in a conversation (about literacy, Sweden has an amazing 99 percent rate). The other two maniacs were listening attentively, nodding and occasionally throwing in a pertinent fact (socialized day care). No one was even smoking and I had totally forgotten about Goal 666 (for our Mexican *hermanos,* Meta Numero Seis, Seis, Seis): Corrupt the World/Spread the Metal!!!

Maniacs, brothers, Vikings: lend me your hellishly buzzing ears. We must labor with guitar and anvil to spread the fire of pure heavy metal! They say entropy is inevitable but we must still toil to ensure the decay progresses! In my own life, only constant vigilance has been able to halt the creep of flowering vines up the balcony of my meager studio apartment. Only a daily regimen of Satanic throat-singing and a pentagram drawn with chicken blood on my doorstep has kept kittens from being born in the backseat of my Camaro, butterflies from deciding my workplace was a bitchin' stop on their migration route, and my neighbor Maria from constantly bringing me hot dishes covered with cloth napkins. My sister always tells me I am a sweetheart, but with effort I find I am not a sweetheart. If I didn't take care, my voice would slip back up to a clear, tenor register and I might find myself humming, on a warm spring day, snatches of show tunes. *I Feel Pretty!* Yet, I've been able to avert the light so that die-hard blacking metal still burns on in the many hatred thrashing parts of my soul! We must not allow beauty to exist without corruption. Listen all maniacs! We must not give up the fight!

Because here's what happened. One afternoon I strolled into practice (still wearing my smock from Speedy Pro, where I'm a reproduction technician) and there, beneath the flaming, Day-Glo painting of the Fallen Angel himself, stood a girl. She had short, bleached hair and a lot of bitchin' ink sticking out of her leather vest, which she wore without a shirt. Pussy is advantageous but should be ornamental in the extreme! This chick was not ornamental, was not our first groupie, because right away I noticed she was perched over a musical instrument. Hold on to your lunch. It was a synthesizer.

Of all the limp-dick instruments in the universe, the synthesizer is the most flaccid. Guys who wear lipstick play synthesizer music for horny little fairies to dance to—I don't need to tell you this. It's well known among bitchin' sons of Lucifer the foul fiend and those Swedish men were well aware of this. Well aware. Anders entered the cement bunker where we practiced our art, his stringy hair swinging about his broad shoulders, and introduced me to the girl. Her name, he said, was Liv. She was from Amsterdam, where she had been a member of an experimental music collective dedicated to bringing microtonal compositions to shut-ins, the institutionalized, and old people. Liv grinned and came out from behind the synthesizer to shake my hand. She wore a short leather skirt and that tiny vest as I mentioned. Her body was tremendous, a fierce combination of soft and athletic, so stunningly proportioned that it could have popped out of a lingerie catalog, but I found her face scrunched and ugly, like a pug's. The overall effect was confusing and for a moment I found I couldn't say anything as Liv sprang behind the synthesizer and began to bang on the keys.

I don't know a lot about synthesizers, but the sounds Liv managed to hack out startled me. Instead of the floaty tones I expected, she produced muscular, ugly noises that reminded me of hooks piercing sheet metal in hell. Then, she flipped some switches and made some other sounds that were like live cats being skewered by white hot knives. Nonetheless I was repulsed, as the synthesizer itself is a sissy instrument and should never be included in a rain of dark riffs. Particularly if played by a female, whose place it is to be soft and pink and stay in her scented room, praying to the moon.

While Liv played she had a big grin plastered on her face; beside her Anders laughed and tapped his foot. They seemed to be having a wonderful time. Then, abruptly, she stopped. "Anders," she called, her odd little face bright with delight, "fetch me my valise!"

Anders obeyed, hustling across the room to grab a small satchel and dropping it at her feet.

"I have brought a gift for you," she announced. She pulled out a record and presented it to me. It was a copy of "Head Abortion," a rare single from Flayed Open, one of my favorite Swedish bands.

"Anders said you needed this. I located it in Europe!" Liv tossed back her head and giggled, and her face softened and spread into a more human countenance. Then she and Anders began to laugh like children, or adults on drugs. I watched them and smirked, fully aware that they were trying to break down my resistance, but the dark power and spirit had made me formidable! Through a careful regimen of self-control I'd become fully immune to joy and could not be seduced by the playful laughter of my bandmates! Liv stumbled and collapsed on top of Anders. Despite the dirt, ash, and dried residue of various liquids on the floor, they began rolling around down there. I think they were having a tickle fight. Her miniskirt edged up and I glimpsed a flash of panty. The next thing I knew, Liv grabbed my leg and pulled me down.

I was beginning to think Liv might make an acceptable groupie, but she could never, ever play in our band.

At a meeting at Pepe Lou's, Anders, our trusted leader, solemnly declared Liv the newest member of Lords of Sludge. Max took the news calmly, grunting slightly and never pausing in his consumption of Tater Tots with ketchup. Max's English skills were rather poor and he rarely said anything anyway. I thought I detected a slight scowl on the face of Stefan, beneath the facial hair that had been spreading and spreading since the day we first met until it covered his entire face, from just below the eyes to the top of his collar. I found this facial hair very werewolf-like and antisocial and approved of it vigorously. As for myself, I sat silently, chewing iceberg lettuce with Russian dressing, rehearsing in my head all the reasons why Liv could not join the band and plotting a scathing delivery for my objections. But before I had a chance to actually offer them, Liv jumped up from the table and began dancing a heavy-metal victory dance, stomping her boots and flashing the double-eared sign of Satan with both hands. "Lords of Sludge," she hooted, "Lords of Sludge!" Her scrunched face turned red with enthusiasm. At the next table, an old lady began to blow a rape whistle.

Liv had a nest of hair in her armpits and I could see it well as she slid into the booth and draped her arm around the cringing crone. "What's wrong, little mother? Have I given you a fright?"

The lady shrank back with the whistle dangling from her mouth. It seemed she regarded Liv with deep suspicion. Max was laughing gleefully at this, as were Stefan and Anders, and I knew my chances of ousting Liv were fading.

"I want not to harm you," she said to the senior, "but to please you. May I kiss your cheek?"

"Don't you dare," the old lady hissed, edging away from the armpit.

"I won't kiss you then, mother. I'm from across the sea and my customs must seem strange."

"Get away," the elderly woman said, but something in her had calmed and she said it without conviction. She'd let the whistle fall back into her purse and started to nibble on her eggs. Liv removed her arm from around the woman and began to chat with her politely, hands clasped in front of her on the table. Like the Swedes, she had lovely manners, and in a few moments Liv had charmed her foe utterly. The two sat chatting softly about whatever it is women talk about; then they were exchanging phone numbers.

After a while Liv bounded back to our table, sprightly-go-lucky, bragging that she had subdued the old one. The Swedish men applauded with delight and piled their extra Tater Tots on Liv's plate. They began an animated discussion about walking clubs for the elderly in different European countries while I slumped in the corner, one lone man, fuming.

The forest is our mother, and we must destroy the forest! When I see pocked mountain slopes, clear-cut of trees, I feel virile, hulking, masterful. When I see the machines of my fellow men chewing through groves in which I played as a child, consuming glens in which I picnicked with my mother and sister when I was a boy, I feel enlarged. We are men, in charge, plowing our masculinity into the earth, and in my heart I'm gladdened those places are destroyed because then I'll never be tempted to return to the dimpled, the pink, the fluffy. A true metal head knows innocence is irretrievable.

And so, to me, it was obvious Liv's femininity would corrupt us, soften us, wash us out to shades of pastel, but I figured if I complained the guys would kick me out of the band. Then where would I be? I'd be a clerk in a copy shop without a band. I'd be another minimum-wage worker in a leather jacket popping into the convenience store on the way home to buy a twelve-pack of beer with wadded bills and a handful of change. I didn't want to leave the rock and roll life. It was just beginning to happen for us. We'd finally managed to schedule a gig, and I was looking forward to playing in front of an audience. Then there was the fact that I loved it. For me there was nothing more satisfying than our give-and-take of energy, the unselfish sharing of talent, skills, and inspiration. When everything was working right, when all of us were in harmony, it was beyond bitchin'.

I was also genuinely fond of the Swedish men and their messy hair and the sauna where we often spent the evenings. Liv began to join us in the sauna as well, and I admit I appreciated the chance to spend time next to a live, naked girl. Now and then she rubbed against me and laughed. She tugged at the towel around my waist and requested to see "the nature of my unit." Later, she and Anders traipsed off to the bedroom together while the rest of us watched television and snacked on pickled herring.

Many nights, after warming in the sauna, we'd go running naked through the woods behind the house. I knew that over the hill was a shopping mall, and next to that a plowed lot where they were putting in a parking tower, but from our vantage point it almost seemed like we were in a primeval forest. When we got tired of running we'd leap backward into the drifts and thrash about, making angels in the snow. Of course, my angel and the angels of the Swedish men were dark and brooding, fallen soldiers of Satan. Twigs, piss, and pine branches helped the effect. But Liv's angels were luminous. No matter how hard she tried to thrash out something sinister, her angels were always feathery. They seemed to float on the snow, and cupped the moonlight like a silver goblet.

"Liv," said I, "you must be a Stardust Woman. You are not of the darkness like us."

Liv laughed and made the double-eared sign of Satan in the air. "You are mistaken, Gabe [for Gabe is my name], I am quite badly bitchin'!" Her silver laughter clogged the air like bubbles. "Dark power," she sang, prancing in the snow. "Dark power to all the children!"

"No," I replied. "Look at your angels. They look real. You are full of light, Liv. You are a good witch."

"She is full of hatred!" Anders insisted, smashing a fist into his palm.

Liv looked at the two of us, then threw her head back and laughed, her short, bleached hair catching the moonlight like a piece of dandelion fluff.

"I do not think," I said, very quietly, shivering in the drifts, "that she is full of hatred."

It was a frosty night, and soon the other men fled back to the sauna. Liv, though, seemed immune to temperature.

She bounced around, licking snow off tree branches, her tiny hands clasped under her chin like a kangaroo. Kangaroos look cuddly but in fact are vicious fighters. I was freezing and my toes were turning blue but I couldn't stop watching her. I admit I sort of liked being alone with her, naked. She had a chance to take a look at the nature of my unit if she wanted, but she seemed more intent on eating snow. The unit was pretty shrunk up from the cold anyway.

Liv bounded between the pines. "I'm pollinating," she said. "I take the snow from tree to tree. I am a pollinator."

"Liv," said I, "you are a freak!"

She bounced over and poked me in the stomach. "You small turd," she whispered. "You are a turd, and I'm a turd too!"

"I beg your pardon?"

"Ha! You try to act mean, but I see what a dumpling you are!"

What an odd, odd, odd, feeling Liv gave me—for a second, when she pronounced the word "dumpling," I was overwhelmed by an urge to grab her hand and skip off into one of those red, dripping sunsets they have on seventies greeting cards. It was an electric, honeymoon feeling, full of fun and frolic and utterly devoid of evil, loathing, or resentment. It was what I feared most—that deep down, in my core of being, I harbored a little flame of light.

I've always wanted desperately to be bad. I've always wanted to be extremely evil, full of hatred. I've always wanted people to exclaim, when I walk into a room: *Look at that fellow! He is truly bad!* Instead of saying what they usually say, which is nothing, or at most *Look at that fellow, he has one of those pointy devil beards like our friend Skizz.* Skizz is not bad; Skizz is a nice guy. I've tried to be self-centered and an asshole; I've tried to follow the path of Satan; I've tried to absorb all the meager boredom and antipathy that's been thrown my way by coaches, teachers, and popular girls and radiate it back, larger, grander, and more corrosive than ever, but I have a set of reflexes I can't control. I have an overwhelming desire to help those in trouble, or to talk to a person at a party if they seem to feel out of place, or to take stray animals home and love them. But I still feel a heavy sense of rejection and ugliness around my person. No one ever talks to me at a party if I feel out of place. No one ever wants to take me home and love me.

Heathens, take heart! Remember, the Vikings sailed the seas to find fresh, new places to invade! We must push ourselves daily to be worthy of the Dark Lord! As I trudged home that dark night from the house of the Swedish men, my boots crunching through the virgin snow, I rededicated myself to the task of corruption. I made a resolution to be as bad as possible. I would take the sparkly things of this world—including Liv, especially Liv—and muddy them. I would be smelly and dirty; of the dark, like a bat.

My resolve only grew stronger as the day approached when we were scheduled to play at Hole in One, a great Metal/Doom bar that had once been a great Golf/Sports bar. We had a show on a Friday night and were very stoked to play hellish great songs dedicated to Satan! In the weeks before the gig, our practices intensified. It became more important than ever that we work together. Hey, I'm no party pooper. I stashed my hatred; I nurtured it like a coal in a bucket of peat, saving it for later, when it would be most effective. This was the time to practice our Black/Doom metal music, including hellish great songs I'd written myself, like "The Bad Watcher Watches" and "Eater of My Soul." I observed Liv's luminous blond head bob and sway during practice; I listened to her synthesizer rumble and croak, and I waited. She would get hers, I thought. I'd really give it to her.

"More melody," Liv said, perched over her keyboard like a pretty songbird. "We must make our music fiery with melody!"

The Swedish men were in complete agreement. I, too, knew that the mighty power of Scandinavian metal music came from its ability to reconcile euphony with discord. Together, under Liv's guidance, we strengthened our songs, making them more tuneful. Liv designed vigorous, bold melodies on her keyboard; they were like the beams and rough-hewn buttresses on which our songs rested. Liv and I had to work especially closely, since lyric and melody go hand in hand. The Swedish musicians devised flourishes that enriched the whole. We started practice at five P.M. and played most nights until eleven. We improved steadily. We ordered pizza. After a while, even on days when we weren't practicing, our songs stuck in my head. It was happening. The Lords were mutating from a great band into an awesome one.

I would guess the Vikings had some sort of ritual they performed before going into battle. Perhaps they danced around a block of ice, or killed a she-goat. As modern-day warriors we had our own ritual of bodily adornment and preparation that we referred to as "getting ready for the gig." This took me quite some time, and it seemed to require a similar amount of effort for the Swedish men, because when I arrived at the club, there they all sat, on time as usual, with their hair teased and lacquered into various startling arrangements. Anders's tattoos were especially dark. His hair was shiny but stringier than ever and I thought I detected a touch of mascara. Stefan had combed his facial hair downward and looked more bestial than any human I'd ever seen; Max was clad entirely in black (okay, we all were) and had polished the silver pentagram around his neck. But of us all, Liv had been the most transformed by her preparations. She wore a boned, black bra that really showed off her figure. On her feet were pink go-go boots, and she'd painted a spiderweb across her cheek that completely camouflaged her canine quality. The truth is she looked beautiful.

I was almost swayed. It occurred to me that Liv was a nice girl with a good disposition and that I might this one time show some mercy—but in my heart I knew I must be fierce! Besides, I'd already decided how to strike. From my little sister I'd learned a foolproof way of wounding girls, and so, mustering all the darkness within me, all the hostility and thrashing evil, I turned to Liv, who was sitting by her synthesizer, polishing the keys, and said, "Wow. That outfit makes you look really fat."

For a moment Liv seemed taken aback. The spiderweb across her face curved downward while she took in my blackening evil countenance, the hatred spewing from within me. She looked at me with her muddy brown eyes, directly into my smoking core.

"Oh, Gabe! You had me going for a minute! Such a

kidder! You're such a lamb." The spiderweb expanded when she giggled.

Then I was onstage, standing in a pool of hot light. I held a microphone in my fist and something was feeding back through the P.A. Anders fiddled with some knobs and the room grew silent except for the creaking of my leather trousers. I felt fuzzy and confused. I shaded my eyes and looked into the audience: not a bad turnout. Maybe a hundred metal heads slumped around in front of the stage; a few skinny girls, but mostly guys with bored faces and long, clean hair and freshly laundered, ripped T-shirts. They seemed to be in various stages of drunkenness. Behind me, Stefan crouched over his drum kit like a feral animal. To my right, Anders stood with his guitar hanging in front of his hips while Max waited expectantly behind his bass. At my side stood Liv, perched over her synthesizer with an elfin sparkle in her eye.

It was silent. I was waiting for something to happen, but nothing happened. I waited to feel malicious and potent but felt light and perky instead. Then, on Liv's count we sprang to life. Max plucked out the throbbing bass line to "The Bad Watcher Watches," an extremely Satanic song—this song makes "Parricide 2" seem like a trip to the petting zoo. Anders joined in with his growling but nonetheless buoyant guitar line. Entwined between was Liv's lilting, sinister melody, which sounded a little like a calliope in a movie about a clown who eats children.

We sounded awesome. It was like we'd been practicing together our entire lives. Every part slid into place and blended with the others, without a thought. The crowd started to churn and wind around itself. I could feel the floorboards vibrating as we played louder, harder; my Satanic throat singing was really featured in this song and I felt the cells peeling off my larynx as I struggled to sing in a deeper, more frightening register: *He watches us / The bad watcher watches us / Ooooo / He watches us / Toil from the mountaintop . . .*

The crowd had begun to gyrate and shake. By the second chorus, they were going totally berserk. So many heads of hair were banging in front of me that the skirt of the stage looked like a field of wheat in a windstorm. I stepped out of the lights to give the other guys a chance to take their solos. Anders began wailing on his instrument as if it were a small animal he hoped to beat to death. He leaned forward and banged his head—his hair was actually getting caught in the strings of his guitar, but he didn't slow down—he was lost in the crunch of the music and the heat of the lights and the smell of the fans sweating below us. He was playing flourishes I'd never heard *anywhere* before, much less from Anders; wild, scrubbing riffs that were nevertheless melodic and tinged with sadness. That his guitar was merely an electrified construction of wire and wood and a couple of old pickups seemed unimaginable—it was more like a fallen angel spewing out the wickedest rock and roll from the lower intestine of hell! I closed my eyes. When I opened them, Anders's fingers were bleeding all over the pick guard.

Then Stefan took a drum solo. He was like a mutant woodland creature with advanced hand-eye coordination; his sticks flew over the kit so quickly they blurred. The kids in the audience stared at him with their mouths open. Then he stopped, hands raised, perspiration gushing down his ribs. All was silent. No one in the crowd so much as hooted. Slowly he brought both hands down at once; bam. Then up and down again. Bam. He was beating a slow rhythm with all his might on the snare, only the snare. Bam, bam, bam—it was trance inducing. It was like caveman music. The crowd loved it. We all loved it.

It was time for Liv to begin her synthesizer solo. Notes as soft as petals hung in the air beside the serrated snarls of a ruthless predator dismembering her prey. Liv's head drooped as her fingers leapt across the keys, urging forth a driving, overwhelming rock and roll moment. How could I have ever called the synthesizer a pansy instrument? The crowd roiled and churned. An odd tingling consumed me as I watched them, a kind of warm numbness. As Liv pushed the tune farther into the realm of the melodious, I began to feel almost ill with a kind of unpleasant pleasure, like being tickled. Something was happening—something was grasping at me; I had a sense it was grasping all of us. I was being swept up by a breezy, harmonious wave of major chords struck with pep. Then, after a weird, underwater period where I thought I might faint, my head cleared, and I understood what was happening.

A melody issued from Liv's organ, a melody effusive and irrepressible. It was contagious. It was sweet. It was Rodgers and Hammerstein's "Happy Talk," from the musical *South Pacific*, and *I* was belting it out. A rich, dulcet tenor sprang from my throat as helplessly I found myself constructing the musical question: *You've got to have a dream! If you don't have a dream! How you gonna have a dream come true?* My mind filled with all the Carpenters songs I had loved and I thought of how I always tried, as a boy singing in the shower, to get my vowels to sound as velvety and overstuffed as Karen Carpenter's did. I couldn't help it then; a tide of pent-up joy washed over me. It was uncontrollable, it was uncool and wrong, and I was *so* happy. I was so happy I felt sick. It was as though all the loathing and resentment I'd been nursing at least since I was a sophomore in high school had burst like a soap bubble, had been popped and defused and dried out, and all that was left inside me was a lather of pure euphoria. I was so happy I thought I might melt.

We were of the light, bedazzling all. Liv arched over her synthesizer, singing, while the Swedes strummed joyfully along. Anders banged out sweet, chiming chords on his guitar, an expression of blank rapture on his face. Max was laughing and bobbing from his knees. We were making something lovely. Together we praised the power of creation. Below, our fans stared, openmouthed with horror. Liv lifted her fingers from the keyboard and began to do the happy talkie dance with both hands.

Sally's Story

I DON'T KNOW if this is a happy story or a sad one, but like all good stories it's true. It's about Sally, a dog we had when I was a girl growing up in Phoenix, Arizona, during the nineteen seventies. Some of you have probably heard of Sally. She was quite famous in her day and was written up in a lot of popular magazines. Even *60 Minutes* was going to do a segment on her, but my dad wouldn't allow it. My dad picked out Sally when she was a puppy, but by the time she was doing her best work he didn't much like her anymore. By then he wouldn't pet her, not even if she put her nose in his lap, which was hard to believe because Sally was an incredibly adorable dog.

She was a greyhound. You weren't really supposed to own greyhounds then because they were bred to chase things, and I think the theory was that they might take off after kids and attack them. But Sally was gentle as a cow. She had some kind of hip problem and so had never been able to run, much less race; my dad got her from a friend of his who was a breeder. My dad was the kind of guy who could always get the things other people couldn't. During the energy shortage, he always took our cars out to fill them up with gas.

In the low light of evening, Sally looked just like a baby deer. She had close-set eyes, round and syrupy, like Bambi's. She had long tapering legs and a flecked, fawn-colored coat. When, as an adult, I learned more about wildlife, I became fascinated by how closely Sally had resembled the dik-dik, a small, antelope-like mammal of the African savanna. There's a stuffed one in the Museum of Natural History nearby. Sometimes in the afternoons when Tasha has the boys, I go to the African gallery and squint at the stuffed dik-diks until they turn into fuzzy versions of Sally, standing motionless in the evening light in our backyard, serene and thoughtful, the way she often was later in her life. I guess I miss her. I think we all do.

In her early days, Sally was a ball dog. In retrospect, it seems that her obsession with the ball was the first sign of what was to come. Nothing in God's creation, no steak or table scrap, fascinated her more than a tennis ball. We had white ones and the then-new yellow ones that phosphoresced in the twilight. My dad had painted a while line on a brick wall in the back of the house and my sister Wendy and I used to go out there with our wooden rackets and hit those glowing yellow balls against the wall in the coolness after sunset. We had to shut Sally in the house if we were hitting balls, otherwise she'd go insane. Apeshit, said my dad. She was like a junkie for tennis balls. She wanted to chase them, and once she had one, she was extremely reluctant to give it back. She'd attempt to clutch three or four balls at once, one or two in her mouth and another scissored between her paws. I remember how she looked, hunkering over a trio, following my movements with those suspicious doe eyes, growling halfheartedly if I came too close. Sometimes my sister Wendy would put all the balls in a drawer and Sally would whine and scratch at the furniture for hours.

It seemed that her mind was completely filled with images of balls, but who knows what she was thinking? She had no medium then. She was obsessed, certainly, but she seemed like an ordinary pet. We loved her, but we didn't really think about her much. Or if we did, we just thought that she was a good dog.

After her accident, Sally started constructing things in the yard. The injury wasn't grave—she got winged by the De Harts' car and had to wear a cast on a hind leg for a few weeks. She hobbled on three legs and had trouble keeping her cast clean. It began to smell of urine. She seemed to have a kind of self-awareness then, when she tottered around the house, sniffing herself constantly as though she had picked up the scent of her own mortality. Maybe it wasn't the accident, or not that event alone, that changed things for her. I suppose Sally always had a lot on her mind.

Shortly after she recovered from her injury, Sally began her life's work. At first, we didn't recognize it as such. My father never did. But quite a few well-respected people in the *rest* of the world are in agreement about the fact that Sally was an artist, even an important one. All I knew was that Sally was collecting things in the deep end of our swimming pool, which had been drained for several years due to an algae problem. The concrete sides of the pool were still a cool, mossy green. Against this Sally made her first assemblage of tennis balls, sticks, palm fronds, and chew toys. She used mud or cat feces to glue her creations together. I believe I was the first human ever to lay eyes on one of Sally's pieces.

I discovered it one afternoon after I had been searching for Sally for about an hour. My sister was inside practicing her makeup application. My mom was probably making dinner. It was overcast. I was ten years old. After calling for Sally all over the neighborhood, I finally heard her tags rustling near the diving board. When I got closer I saw her standing in the bottom of the pool, just standing, staring at her incredible construction. It was a sort of bower, nest-like but less functional than any nest. I remember the spray of dark palm fronds fanned against the minty ground of the algae-stained concrete, and the white spiral of tennis balls coiling at its base. Wedged between the balls were sticks Sally had scavenged from the yard. In the center, like a mauled and nesting hen, was Sally's favorite rawhide chew toy.

I climbed down the steps and stood with her, petting her head. She turned and looked at me, happily, but there was something different about her. She seemed distant. I wondered if she might be sick. I'm embarrassed now when I recall my first words to Sally after laying eyes on that miraculous sculpture. I believe I said: "Go get the ball, girl. Go get the ball."

Sally stared at me, incredulous. She parted her lips and began to pant. I went over and removed a tennis ball from the coil and flung it across the yard. Sally watched it sail away sadly. She lowered herself onto her belly and gazed at me with wet, reproachful eyes. I picked up another ball. Sally started to whine.

I went into the house and told my mom Sally was sick.

From that day forward, Sally continued her work in the backyard. My mom told me that Sally was fine, and that there was nothing to worry about as long as her nose felt damp. No one else in my family seemed especially concerned. My dad said Sally probably had some peculiar behavior because she was a sighthound who had been bred for her special qualities since ancient times. He seemed proud of this, as though he had somehow contributed to the breeding process himself.

On hot afternoons, I'd sometimes come across some small artifact of Sally's: a curve of half-buried tennis balls slithering across the yard, or an odd collection of leaves partially scattered by the wind. I believe Sally was still learning about materials then and some of her constructions didn't survive long. Still, I stumbled across some amazing sights—a trampled circle of grass, glossy and blond, with two wooden triangles inside, connected at the points like angel's wings. In the center of each triangle, Sally had placed a spool of cat feces.

That particular construction was the first to be photographed by Betsy Blenman, a friend of my mother's and a curator at the Heard Museum. She was the first official "art world" person to see Sally's work. "Discover" is a word I've also heard used, of Betsy's support of Sally's work, but that seems inaccurate. Maybe "stumbled upon" is best. It was during a backyard barbecue when Betsy lowered one of her high heels into the center of Sally's piece. I had become quite a fan of Sally, by then, and I tried frantically to keep Betsy from destroying one of my favorites.

"Is this your little dollhouse, honey?" I recall Betsy as being the kind of woman who treated all children as if they were toddlers. "Does your mommy let you play with poopie?"

I informed her that I had nothing to do with it. I told her Sally had constructed the area in question. Betsy seemed impressed.

Of course, it was only when I was older that I learned Betsy had been the first to publicize Sally's work. At the time, I only knew that strangers began to take an interest in our backyard. I remember bearded men, in jackets that smelled of pipe smoke, crouching down in the weeds. I remember women in wool skirts, wearing gigantic Indian necklaces, taking Milk-Bones from fringed handbags and slipping them to Sally.

Sally bore all this with quiet dignity. She would pad after our visitors, watching them examine her work, sniffing their fingers if they were offered and allowing herself to be petted if necessary. Sally had lost the frantic, prancing energy she had when she was younger. She was focused. Even to me, a little girl, it was clear that Sally had a purpose—that she had work. My own mother was a housewife, and though the labor she did as a caretaker was certainly important, it garnered her none of the respect and status Sally's efforts earned her. I've always been grateful that, at that tender age, I had a role model like Sally in my life. Of course, she was a dog, but that distinction seemed not to have been particularly sharp in my mind. I knew that Sally was female, and I knew that her work had meaning, to the world at large, and to herself.

Interest in Sally's work began to build. My mom had a collection of articles—from scientific magazines at first, and later from glossy art publications. A couple of film crews visited from news shows. They wanted to shoot Sally at work, but she was decidedly private, and they found it difficult to catch her in action. As a result, the crews tended to stick around the house for days, drinking my mother's coffee, eating her cottage cheese, watching Sally while she slept on the rug. I liked finding them there when I came home from school. Their equipment seemed impossibly official—the cameras, the rolls of tape, the big boom microphones. They were mostly young men, and I was fascinated to see how much they seemed to like my pretty, personable mom. They laughed at her jokes and complimented her food. I loved her even more when I had a chance to see that other people appreciated her too.

My father, however, didn't appreciate all the attention. He grew aloof around Sally and complained that she smelled of cat shit. I remember one evening when the whole family had just sat down to dinner. Sally had just finished arranging herself on the kitchen rug, lowering herself with a groan because of her hip problem, when my dad made his announcement. He looked at us defiantly, like he was going to lay down some new family rule, such as—No Talking on the Phone After Nine P.M. But what he said was: "That dog is a freak of nature. I don't care what anybody else thinks. There's something wrong with that dog."

Sally raised her head and sniffed. I threw her a little ball of hamburger, even though I wasn't supposed to.

"Daddy," argued my sister, "I thought you loved Sally."

My father had his forearms on the table, a fork in one hand and a knife in the other—my big, handsome father with his Superman jaw and his head of blond hair, who made waitresses blush when he called them "honey." He looked at me, he looked at Wendy, and he looked at my mother. "Three women," he said with disgust. "Four if you count Sally. Four against one."

Then he resumed eating. I thought that would be that. But it was only the beginning. The next day he came home carrying a box with holes punched in it. He herded us into the living room. Sally was outside and he insisted we call her in too. "She's one of the family," he said. My dad seemed happy, but not in a real way—he had acted like this when he crashed my mom's car. I guess he was excited by the prospect of what might happen next. He asked Wendy to open the box. Even now, Wendy says she had no idea what was inside, and I can't believe it. It felt like we all knew exactly what was there.

It was a greyhound puppy. She was four weeks old, hardly big enough to be weaned. My father could hold her entire squirming body in the palm of one hand. She slid out of the box, lumpy, shivering, and helpless, and burrowed herself into my sister's lap. Wendy picked her up and kissed her. Later, because of her gray coloring, and not anticipating the ribbing she would get from her pothead friends a little farther into adolescence, Wendy named the puppy Smoke.

I was stunned. I looked at my mother. She was frowning and shaking her head. Sally had retreated to the corner of the living room, beyond the light of the lamp. I couldn't quite see her face, but I felt that she was perturbed. Sally had been spayed when she was about ten months old, and must have never expected to find herself, at this point in her life, living with a puppy.

My father urged her over. "Come here, girl. Come meet your little niece." He had the same aura about him that he had on Christmas morning, very bright and cheerful—so much so that he didn't seem to notice the disapproval in my mother's voice when she asked him if he thought the puppy was a good idea for Sally.

"Sally will love her," he said. "That yard work of hers, it's just misplaced maternal energy. Now she can be a mommy."

This was the seventies, remember, and even though my mother was a housewife, she knew all about women's lib. "Maybe Sally doesn't want to be a mommy," my mother said. "Maybe she wants to be an artist."

"We'll see," he said grimly.

The puppy had to be bottle-fed. My dad wasn't the type of father to get involved in such things, but he encouraged Wendy (I would have nothing to do with it) to coax Sally into being present at the feedings. He tried to get the two dogs to curl up together, going so far as to physically transport Smoke, when she was sleeping, and nestle her next to Sally. Sally, for her part, looked at the puppy. She just looked at it. Whenever they were in a room together, Sally would stare at the puppy, not with affection, but with a deep and abiding suspicion. She treated that puppy the way some people treat the homeless—with subtle tactics of avoidance. When my dad would nestle the sleeping puppy beside her, she would freeze, panting with stress, and then carefully, almost in slow motion, raise herself up and slink away. I'd find her later outside, eating grass.

The puppy sometimes followed Sally around, but in general it seemed Smoke was too stupid to form any true attachments. Nonetheless, she was frisky and wanted to play. She harassed poor Sally for hours, nipping at her muzzle, chasing her tail, trying to entice her into a rousing game of tag. Sally moved smoothly in the presence of Smoke, in a sort of slow, oozing glide—hoping, I believe, to appear uninteresting. It was to no avail. No matter how sloth-like Sally was in her movements, Smoke was still inspired to hurl her little body into Sally's bigger one, over and over, with great hilarity. Sally had a look about her of desperate tolerance, then. In retrospect, it seems to me that she looked like she needed a martini.

To my great disappointment, Sally's work began to suffer. Smoke mistook Sally's craftsmanship for play, and tried to "help" by tugging at her pieces. Some interested parties had given Sally a variety of raw materials, including rubber balls, lengths of cloth, clay, cans of Campbell's tomato soup, even little clusters of hippie bells. Sally used some of these and ignored others, but Smoke had a habit of tearing up anything she found in a pile. In some ways, Smoke and Sally possessed opposing aesthetics. Sally's aesthetic led her to create a lyric order from the natural world. She took objects that were beautiful to her and juxtaposed them in ways that seemed to heighten their poignancy, to create transcendent meaning. Smoke, on the other hand, liked to seek out neatly ordered areas and decimate them.

Even I had no way of knowing how much of Sally's work Smoke destroyed. Sally sometimes allowed me to observe her process, but she preferred to work in private, and it's possible that Smoke chewed up many of her pieces before they were ever beheld by human eyes. Really, I think Sally wasn't that interested in who viewed her work, human or otherwise. She handled her growing fame with a grace that bordered on indifference; she didn't seem to actually *need* an audience. She was a pure artist. She created for the sheer joy of it, for the satisfaction. Though I believe she did hope her creations would last for a short while; long enough, at least, for her to enjoy them.

I remember a row of gourds scattered on the ground beneath our rusted swing set. Sally had swathed and partially buried every other one in a layer of red cloth, in a gesture that prefigured (and perhaps influenced) Christo's work. Day after day Sally and I would slip outside at sunset and watch the fading light playing over the shapes. I, too, found this piece unspeakably beautiful. I would look at the gourds, and I would look at Sally watching them, panting in the summer heat, clear drops of liquid rolling off the end of her tongue. She would raise one eyebrow, then the other, back and forth, over and over, proud and mournful. I think they spoke to her. I think she found her meaning there.

Smoke tore up the gourd piece and many others that summer.

The gourd piece was punctuated at each end by a mound, fashioned when Sally had dug a hole in the typical doggy fashion. This work heralded her period of mound-based earthworks. It was early that fall when I found her first complete earth sculpture, the one whose photograph appears in the 4th edition of Janson's *History of Art.* It was simple, almost abstract: a large pile of dirt, surrounded at the base by a ring of small, blue stones

(Sally, in a painstaking process, had crawled through a hole in the fence and swiped these from a neighbor's yard). In the center of the mound was an indentation. Cradled inside was the small, lifeless body of Smoke.

My father said right away that Sally killed Smoke. He went through the house screaming it, actually, while my mother followed anxiously behind carrying a dustpan as though he were trailing crumbs. Painful as this is to admit, I was inclined to agree with him. It was unclear how Smoke had died, but there were marks on her body indicating violence. Sally was big enough, and she certainly had a motive. And though there was something mournful, even reverent about *Smoke's Mound* (it introduced a still-raging debate among anthropologists over whether or not animals are capable of ritual disposal of their dead), it looked incriminating for Sally.

Of course, I can see now who else would have had a motive to murder Smoke.

My mom, at the time, was undergoing a transformation I recognize now as being typical of women of her class and generation during that era. She had stopped going to the hairdresser and had started to wear beaded earrings. She gave up her starched white shirts for halter tops. She remained, in essence, a housewife, but at the same time she began to develop other interests. On Wednesday afternoons she took a community college pottery course. She was building a kiln off of the patio. Increasingly, the world at large seemed to hold promise and meaning for her. She started buying records by rock and roll bands with names I found sinister, like Blood, Sweat, and Tears.

She still functioned in a domestic sphere, but the domestic sphere alone had grown too cramped for my mother. She wanted to find herself. She wanted to be a citizen of the world.

This drove my dad crazy. He hated it when he came home and something was different. One time my mom was burning incense and he just about lost a lung coughing. He accused her of smoking dope. My mom was the flexible type and laughed it off, but I think my father was deeply unsettled by the changes in the household. I think he looked around for someone to blame and found Sally.

I will never know for certain if Sally killed Smoke, or if my father did it in an attempt to discredit or hurt Sally, or if she died in some other way. I only know that in one of those ironic twists of fate, the body of Smoke propelled Sally nose-first into the art world. Her earthworks made her a star. It wasn't long before Sally was represented by the Leo Castelli Gallery in New York. Museums all over the world were calling, asking if Sally was available to do installations. My mother and Sally traveled the world to meet the demand for her pieces. All Sally required was a room full of dirt, or a quiet yard, and some privacy to create her wonderful, mounded sculptures, with their Zen-like simplicity and sense of balance. Though much has been said about the calm harmony of Sally's work during this period, it has always had the feel of the reliquary, for me. When I traveled to Italy with Sally and my mother, and saw her series of receding mounds vanishing into the dimness of the sculpture garden at the Venice Biennale, my thoughts gravitated toward Smoke. The smallest mound was just big enough to have covered her body at the time of her death.

My father bought a Ferrari. He'd go out in the middle of the night to "drive around." After I was in bed, I'd hear the growl of the engine start up in the garage, then fade off as he sped away from our house. I was in high school by then and affected bored disinterest in the activities of my parents, perhaps more so because it was obvious my dad was falling apart. He had always liked being in the know, but this had begun to take on a shadowy cast. He brought home strange friends—guarded, heavy men wearing rings and pastel suits. They'd hold conferences in the garage, standing around, staring into the Ferrari. My sister said they were gamblers.

He and my mom fought all the time. He called Sally a bitch and said she was ruining his fucking life, things like that. He complained that my mother was never home anymore. They used to argue in their bedroom with the door closed, but they were so loud that you could hear them all the way in the kitchen. For a while my mom *did* curtail her travels with Sally, but something in my mother had changed too, and it wasn't going to change back. Even when she wasn't helping Sally with her career, she had interests of her own. She had fallen heart and soul for pottery—the lovely planters and ashtrays that she fired in the kiln in the backyard. She gave them to friends or sold them at craft fairs.

The last time I laid eyes on my father, he was standing in our kitchen, feeding baloney to Sally. I had just come home from school and was surprised to see him in the middle of the day. I said hello and got some milk from the refrigerator. He barely glanced at me. Sally sat at his feet, alert and grinning, watching his hands rip up the baloney. "You're a good dog, Sally," he said, popping a shred of lunch meat into her mouth, "you're a good dog." He hadn't talked to Sally for years. He had dark circles under his eyes and his shirt was dirty. He looked old to me, tired and descending down the far slope of middle age.

"Jenny," he said, using the name he'd called me when I was a little girl, "Sally's a good dog."

"I know," I said.

"She's a good dog," he said, "but she's *just a dog.*"

"I know, Dad."

"She's just a dog." He kept saying it, "she's just a dog," with shocked wonder, as though he couldn't believe a four-legged animal could make him feel so small in his own home.

My mom told me later that he took most of Sally's money when he left—more than a hundred thousand dollars. It wasn't just Sally's money either; it belonged to the whole family. I couldn't understand how my father, who had loved us and taken care of us, who had hired clowns for our birthday parties and given us piano lessons, could suddenly stop caring about us because of *anyone*—canine, human, whatever. If Sally had been a dog-headed Fury sent from the gods to wreak havoc on our family, his abandoning us still wouldn't have made sense to me. How could anyone make him hate himself so much?

After he left, Sally continued to influence our lives. My mother traveled and kept up her pottery. Wendy and I both went to private colleges, tuition courtesy of Sally. Wendy became a nutritionist and started having babies right after graduation. I think she wanted to re-create the sense of family we lost when my dad left. I studied art history at Vassar and returned to Arizona after I graduated, perhaps in an attempt to recapture some of the meaning

Sally once brought to my life. I'm not really sure why I came back, but I do know I love it here. I work as a curator for the gallery at the Desert Museum part time, and the twins are almost four.

After my dad left and Wendy went away to school, a quiet intimacy sprang up between Sally and me. The house felt half-empty then. My mom brought home only two or three bags from the grocery store, instead of seven or eight. I felt as though my life as an adult was about to begin, but for the time I was suspended in the cusp between being a daughter and being a woman. I spent that time in front of the television, dieting and painting my nails, steeling myself for what was ahead. Sally was often at my side.

By then Sally was about eleven years old. She'd stopped mounding quite suddenly—just gave it up with no explanation about a year after my father left. For months she padded around the house, sniffing the baseboards, pawing at cupboards. It reminded me of when Wendy used to hide Sally's tennis balls, back when Sally was just a ball dog. Then for a time, Sally became more canine than she had ever been—almost wolfish. She took up howling. Sally had hardly even barked before, but she began spending hours in the backyard, listening for fire trucks. When she heard one she'd tilt her little nose into the air and howl along with it, mouth pursed, eyes half-closed, like an actress in a pornographic film. I thought she was lonely. I thought she was trying to recapture an animal part of herself that she had lost or set aside. But then, I guess I never really knew what Sally was thinking.

Her last works were a sort of simple, direct fusion of dance and sculpture and drama that utilized the basic palette that first drew her to art: the tennis ball, the backyard, and herself. Performance art was in its infancy then; I don't think any of us understood what Sally was up to. She was always ahead of her time.

Very few outsiders witnessed these pieces, though of course, I was in a privileged position to do so. One morning I noticed Sally was making a circle out of tennis balls on a patch of grass in the yard. She arranged them with her mouth, walking back a few paces to assess the effect after she'd placed each one. When she had the circle just so, she sat on her haunches in the center, facing the patio. For the rest of the afternoon she remained there, watching her shadow creep over the balls as though she were the indicator on a sundial. She left once or twice to lap up some water or pee, but for most of the day she sat and watched light and shadow as they played across a series of circles.

I spent much of the day watching too. I came to understand that Sally was a part of her creations now. The restlessness, the obsessive sniffing of cupboards and door handles—all that had stopped. She had found a form that satisfied her. The presence that was in her body flowed through her art; it was in the tennis balls, and it was in the light that played over them all. Matter and spirit had become joined. She was the artist, and she was the art itself. This was the genius of the final work of our beloved greyhound Sally.

Late in my senior year, Sally wheeled herself around on the carpet, tucked herself into a ball, yawned off to sleep, and never woke up. Wendy came home from college for a week. We buried Sally in the backyard, next to one of her mounds.

My father never returned. When I think of all that I learned from Sally—about dignity and dedication, about symmetry and beauty, and how affection can survive loss, and how nature is within us as well as without—I feel so grateful. I feel so lucky to have known and loved her. And I wish I'd never seen her little fawn face. I wish she'd wrecked some other family.

The First Men

I'M RIDING UP an escalator with Roxy explaining how she's the worst mother in the world. Some of my students, I say, have really bad mothers, but she takes the cake. Roxy, who's a real cunt, says something along the lines of "you ungrateful whore" and storms off to Ship 'n' Shore, which is retailese for Fat and Ugly.

I go to the Ladies' Lounge and vomit then proceed to Lingerie to buy a couple of push-up bras on credit. Look, it isn't my fault that Teddy drinks too much, okay? I just want to say that. EVERYBODY ACTS LIKE EVERYTHING IS MY FAULT AND IT ISN'T MY FAULT. I hate it, hate it, hate it. And I wanted that perfume, that's why I lifted it. What do you want me to say? That it's a disease? I have news for you, baby. Greed is not a disease.

A little later, an ugly clerk at the Sunglass Hut is explaining why these three-hundred-dollar glasses are ultimately *me* when Roxy swoops past with her nose in the air, jingling her car keys so I'll notice she's leaving without me. She wants me to run after her, but I'm not going to give her the satisfaction—I mean, is this any way to treat your own daughter? I'm stranded with no nutritional options but corn dogs, frozen yogurt, and the giant cinnamon buns that stink up all the stores west of The Gap. I've maxed out most of my cards. I am not drunk, I haven't scored in several days, nor have I been laid. I'm considering trying to go easy on drugs because of the children. Think of the children! That's what Roxy says, but give me one good reason why I should listen to her.

Besides, I do think of the children. Right now I'm thinking of Roger Wells, everyone calls him Pig Pen—cute. He's in my third period Health Ed class, and he sells me downers at a reduced rate in exchange for a guaranteed B+. This was a good deal for everyone until Pig Pen started skipping class entirely. How am I going to buy drugs when he won't fucking come to class? "It's no big deal, Miss Roberts. Whatever you say, Miss Roberts." That kid is a liar and a degenerate—B+ or not, I'm filling in the negative comment bubbles with a number two pencil on that one. I am TRYING to teach a unit on reproduction, very touchy vis-à-vis the school board, the PTA, the textbook company, and there are only so many things I'm authorized to say according to state law. I keep repeating *abstinence, abstinence* when Pig Pen slinks in late and tosses a note on my desk that says I owe him big money. Through the window, I get a peek at his drones circling. This kid is a really bad kid.

You want to know how they get that bad? Some are born bad. Some of them have bad parents. Some of them watch too much MTV and it spoils them. You can spot the ones that have been corrupted by heavy metal music from the slogans on their T-shirts and their constant, vulture-like slouch. Some of them have been in accidents and received blows to the head. When they wake up, they're bad. Pig Pen may have been bad due to any of these influences, or he may have gone bad during a gym class trauma—getting picked last for a year, pantsing, taunts concerning penis size. It's been known to happen. One day they're little boys and girls, and the next they're criminals and drug addicts.

After the bell rings I tell Pig Pen I need a few days to get the money together, and would he please get me some more of those good downers? For a while he had a pharmaceutical source and could obtain the best, best shit, and when I looked at him I swear I almost started to drool. Pig Pen said Okay, Miss Roberts.

God's honest truth, I was going to pay the kid. Good, bad, I didn't care, he had what I needed. Unfortunately I had to go and drop in on Roxy and have my entire head screwed up, a task that took her about twenty minutes. She's sitting in her kitchen, in a warm-up suit patterned after the British flag, trying to make me eat a pound cake. She's accusing me of having an eating disorder and keeps saying, "Let me look in your mouth, let me look in your mouth," as though I'm a farm animal she's thinking of buying. Then she puts a slice of cake with whipped cream and strawberries in syrup in front of me—a sort of witch test. If I don't eat it, I'm mentally sick. If I do, I'll turn into a fat slug like her.

I pick up the fork. Roxy informs me that I am a heathen, and that I have picked up the wrong fork. I pick up another fork. She sighs and wedges her lumpy hips more firmly in her chair, but after thirty-two years of this I'm certain that this fork is the one. I cut the cake into bite-sized pieces. I consume it daintily. I wait until she's running the insinkerator before I duck into the bathroom to vomit.

After that, she starts whining that we never go anywhere together so we make a date to go to the mall on Saturday. My friend Wanda won't talk to me anymore, but when she did, she used to say WHY DO YOU SPEND SO MUCH TIME WITH THAT WOMAN IF SHE DRIVES YOU CRAZY? But what she doesn't understand is that Roxy has accused me of taking her boyfriend Teddy out drinking when the truth is Teddy is an alcoholic and doesn't need anyone to "help" him drink. We went to the Golden Nugget once or twice, but HE called ME and asked for a ride. Shit. Do you want to know why I'm bad? My mother made me this way.

The upshot is that after the cake incident I was so stressed out I went to Rossingham's and bought four gold chains and a cubic zirconia tennis bracelet with instant credit and a small down payment. I have Roxy to thank for this little spree. The next thing I know it's already Saturday and I'm broke, stranded at the mall, pausing in the food court to watch captive sparrows pecking crumbs off the floor. I think the smell lures them through the automatic doors and the poor things are too stupid to figure out how to get out. Or maybe it's the greatest deal; maybe for a sparrow the mall is the lap of luxury, like living in the Hyatt for a human.

So I'm bird watching and calmly sipping my Diet Coke when I look up and who should be approaching? Not Pig Pen, thank God, but one of his worker drones, Seymour Jackson, to whom I'd given a D the year before in biology.

Seymour Jackson is a big white kid with a military crew-cut and arms that reach almost to his knees. He has the deadened, blank face of a jock but Seymour is not a jock because he's a bad boy and a drug dealer who smokes cigarettes incessantly. In class, he'd chew tobacco and spit into a Big Gulp cup that he liked to balance on the edge of my desk on his way out. Those of Seymour's peers not too frightened to refer to Seymour at all refer to Seymour as "Action."

The way it goes for high school teachers these days is you generally don't want to chitchat with kids you've given a D, particularly strapping lads who work for an organization to whom you owe money for narcotics. Nevertheless, Action Jackson comes right up to me and looks at me—just looks. Very mean. Very tall.

"Miss Roberts?" He seems confused.

"What can I do for you, Seymour?"

"You're at the mall?"

Let me tell you a little bit about these kids. They're not bright. They sniff nail polish remover and drive around with handguns tucked under their registration slips. They wear sunglasses in the rain and get gum stuck in their braces. In my class they think it's really funny to act like retarded mental idiots when I call on them. There are no class clowns anymore—the youth of today are too dim-witted for wisecracking. When I see the instructions "shake and pour" on a carton of orange juice I think Thank God, because these kids are in desperate need of instruction. So I say to Action, enunciating clearly: "Yes, Seymour. I *am* at the mall."

He's drumming his hands on his stomach, rolling his head around in a weak imitation of Stevie Wonder.

Teenage boys, Jesus Christ. They can't hold still for a second and they can't look you in the eye. You can practically smell the hormones steaming from them—it's repellent, but at the same time it's a struggle not to take them home and fuck their brains out. I AM NOT referring to Brandon Murray here. Brandon Murray is a pathological liar who is "at risk" and any charges he's made against me should be regarded as impeachable fantasy.

Then Action wants to sit down. "Miss Roberts, Miss Roberts, can I sit here a minute?" What am I supposed to say? I am thinking this kid might have a gun in his jeans. I owe seven bills and some change to Pig Pen, which isn't all that much, considering these guys drive Camrys and carry cell phones in their backpacks, but they watch a lot of TV, a lot of movies, and they've picked up all manner of bullshit about loyalty, manhood, honor, prompt payment.

"Miss Roberts." He tosses a pack of cigarettes on the table, then his backpack, then a clump of keys with a little pot leaf on the ring. "That book you made me read, the one about the cavemen . . ."

"They're called Homo erectus, Seymour."

"Homo whatever. Look, I know I didn't pay attention in class, but I keep thinking about it. The whole thing about him hunting giant tree sloths and adapting and working in groups . . ." Action's foot is going up and down as if it were electrified. It's possible he's on speed, but he's so hyper to begin with it's hard to tell. He's puffing a cigarette too, pinching the filter really hard, like he wants to prevent it from escaping. "I keep thinking," he says, "about the acquisition of language."

"Hey, Action. Do you have anything for me?"

"Like what?"

"Something powdered. Or in capsule form."

Action drums on the tabletop. He's moving so much of his body in such a fitful manner that looking at him is like watching something under a strobe light. "I can't do it, Miss Roberts," he finally says. "Pig Pen says you gotta pay up first."

"What are you on right now? Can you get some for me?"

"Right now?"

"Yeah, right now."

"Okay," he says. "Wait here."

Action walks around to the other side of the carousel, by the booth where they sell personalized Barbie books imprinted with your child's name. It looks like he's talking on his cell phone, but I'm not sure. I'm thinking that if I manage to escape with my life, I might go to Dillard's and buy some Lancôme eye shadow in smoky gold. Also, if I manage to escape with my life as well as score some drugs, I'll buy a pound of chocolates and eat them without vomiting.

After a few minutes Seymour comes back with a Styrofoam cup in each hand. As he walks across the food court, I detect a bulge under his left arm, through his warm-up jacket. This is bad news. Seymour occasionally seems nice and vulnerable, like a kid, but the truth is he's too young to understand how dangerous he is. It's too bad Roxy ditched me, because I should have already made an exit myself.

"Here you go, Miss Roberts." Seymour places a Styrofoam cup in front of me and tucks his long arms under the table. The cup is half full of black liquid.

"What is this?"

"Espresso. Rocket fuel of the gods."

"That's all you've got for me?"

"Hey. It's stronger than you think."

"Seymour, I have to go now." I gather my bags. Action scoots his chair over to my side of the table and touches my arm—very gentle. Very soothing.

"You can't go just yet, Miss Roberts. You gotta wait awhile."

"Why?"

"You gotta answer me about Homo erectus, okay? I read that First Man book and it was freaking me out." He's leaning toward me, suddenly calm, patient. There's something almost paternal about him. "I mean, it says that in monkeys, feelings go straight into the brain, right? Like an injection."

"There's something called the limbic system, Seymour. Fear, pleasure, pain."

"The reptile brain!"

"Sorta, right. Seymour, I have to go."

"Wait." His hand is on my knee, not in a sexy way, but in an anchoring one. "Homo erectus—he added another step. Like, a filter, right?"

"More or less. Speech centers. Symbolic thinking. Like, if I say the word 'cup' you can think of a generic cup, this cup on the table, whatever, and your brain sorts through the possibilities and figures out what I'm talking about. Ta-da, you've got language. You and I communicating. Understand?"

"And this is like, an amazing leap, right? That book said it took a million years."

"Fuck, Seymour. I don't know how long it took. I wasn't there."

Seymour's big face goes slack. He's disappointed, but what did he want me to say? I'm not even trained in science but the district is so strapped that half of us cross-teach. My field is Spanish and I'm a licensed family counselor. For some reason the district has declared I'll teach health, biology, and remedial math. I am, however, familiar with the book Seymour is referring to, *The First Men*, a title in the Time-Life series I assign as extra credit when a student is failing because it has a lot of pictures. It also happens to have been written by Edmund White, father of the gay literary renaissance and author of a great biography of Jean Genet, a bad boy if ever there was one. If he could ever learn French, I'm sure Seymour would have gotten along great with Jean Genet.

His cell phone is ringing. "Will you please excuse me?" The more polite Action is, the more I figure I'm in trouble. He turns away but keeps his foot on top of my shoe—I have to pretend to ignore this. The more I act like everything is cool, the more likely it is that everything WILL be cool. I'm beginning to think, however, that I'm not going to score any drugs off Seymour on this particular day.

He's on the phone saying *uh-huh, uh-huh.* The way he looks at me with one eye, his body tense but motionless—it's giving me a chill. It's as though every trace of the little boy has been precipitated out of him and what remains is cool and gray. He reminds me of a pair of stiletto heels I tried on in Dillard's. When was that? Less than an hour ago.

"Okay," he says, hanging up the phone. "You're going to have to come with me, Miss Roberts."

"I have a lot of people waiting for me upstairs. My ex-husband. He's a cop."

"You're going to have to hook up with them later, Miss Roberts. I'm really, really sorry about this."

There's a car and then another car parked by a Dumpster. Action nods at a pair of kids I haven't had in my class and urges me into the back of an Econoline van, license plate PMD 525. The two guys in front look like brothers—weak chins, slicked hair, sunken cheeks smothered in clumps of cystic acne. Both are so thin that their bones show through their clothes, but it's not like I could take them. They would have weapons.

"You boys," I ask, "do you go to Salpointe?"

They are not saying anything to me. They are not even turning around and acknowledging that I've spoken.

Action climbs in the back beside me and encourages me to buckle up. I feel he wants this not for safety, but to hold me immobile.

"Hey," I say, "I can get some stuff for your face that'll give you the complexion of a baby—my esthetician makes it. You can't buy it in stores."

The boy in the passenger seat twists around and fixes me with dull, sleepy eyes. His face looks like it got pinched by the forceps on the way out, and right where the tongs would have gone, there's a particularly nasty jumble of welts and pus.

"Miss Roberts," says Action, "would you mind keeping quiet?"

"This stuff is a miracle. If you boys hurt me, you'll throw away any chance of ever clearing up your skin."

"Hey, Miss Roberts . . ." Action sounds pissed.

"And I know how devastating acne can be for kids your age. Okay. I'm through."

The boys start up the van and it feels like we're driving in circles. I can't see outside because the windows are covered with aluminum foil, though I could see through the windshield if Action would scoot over. Action is on the phone again. He's calm, gliding in his movements, and I know this isn't good. He whispers something to the driver, then turns to me.

"We've gotta go see Pig Pen, okay, Miss Roberts? You've gotta give him the money now, today."

"Give me the phone, Seymour."

"I'm not allowed."

"Give it to me or else you're expelled."

"I got expelled already."

"I can get you back in. Seymour. Are you listening to me?"

"It's not my choice, Miss Roberts. We got certain agreements between us. We use language to make agreements in order to do business. We're working together like Homo erectus did to hunt the woolly mammoths. I'm right about that, aren't I?"

"Yes, Seymour."

"You didn't know I was smart, did you?"

"You're a very bright boy."

"Then why'd you give me the D?"

"Because you didn't do the reading, you didn't take the tests, you didn't come to class. You left tobacco spit on my desk. Seymour, look at me." Seymour has started to vibrate again, subtly, in the fingers and feet. "I don't have the money."

The van is no longer traveling in circles. We could easily be out in the desert. People die in the desert all the time—hikers, thieves, Mexicans dodging Immigration. They find them days, weeks, or years later, beneath paloverde trees, huddled in pathetic disks of shade.

"Do you want to go to the prom? I could get you back into school. Take whoever you want."

Action scratches his ear and stares at the foil over the window. After a minute he lights up another cigarette. "Miss Roberts," he says, "I gotta ask you this thing about evolution. Millions of years of things building up—fire, language, hunting, society. I mean, all those stone tools, people trying to form words and their mouths aren't big enough or something. It all builds up to what? To me, like, riding in this van, talking to you?"

"Listen, Seymour. I don't have the money."

He looks away and pats at his hair cautiously, as though it were a toupee. "I know that, Miss Roberts."

"Call my mother—Roxy Ingram. She'll pay Pig Pen."

"Pig Pen already spoke to Roxy, Miss Roberts. She said she wasn't going to pay your debts no more. She said to tell you."

The van makes a right. After a while the ride turns bumpy and I'm almost certain we're on a dirt road. The sun pouring in the windshield is very bright. We all rock from side to side in our seats, the four of us looking very crisp, all the stains on our clothes visible, all of our wrinkles and pimples standing out in the light as though we were under a microscope, being examined for the defect that keeps our mothers from loving us.

"The thing that bothers me, though"—Action's eyes list sideways to some pensive arena—"is what it means. You know? Man evolving from guys with big jaws and shit—is that, what, science? $x = y$ or whatever? Or is it some kind of a miracle?"

Action is a handsome kid. His skin is dewy and he works out at the gym I guess because his arms are big and he doesn't have that inchoate, half-formed look a lot of juniors have. There's something oddly beautiful about the way he can't sit still and can't complete a thought and can't finish exhaling before he inhales, and even though it's likely he'll spend most of his life in jail, and fucking deserves it, at this point in his development it seems entirely obvious that he's a wonder of creation anyway—graceful and predatory, like a shark.

"Yeah, Seymour, I think it's a miracle. I think it's a miracle and a marvel that you've evolved to the point where we can sit here discussing evolution, even as you're driving me out to the middle of nowhere to stab me or shoot me or suffocate me with a couch cushion."

"Ha!" He sucks on his cigarette with deep satisfaction. "I thought so. I thought I was a miracle."

Action leans against the door so I can finally see outside. We're in the desert, clipping past saguaro and cholla, weird plants that look like freaks of evolution themselves. At least I can see the sky, rushing toward us, so blue I feel like if I took a swipe at it, pigment would come off on my hand.

"It's not just you, Seymour," I say. "It's me. I'm a miracle too."

He isn't listening. He's making funny noises with his mouth that are probably meant to mimic an electric guitar. I think the song is "Back in Black." Also, he's playing a set of air drums and vibrating his knees, both of them, up and down with astonishing speed. I rip the foil off the window. We're moving through a valley carpeted with beautiful, thorny plants, about half of them dead. There's a different time scale in the desert; things move slowly. Saguaro don't sprout their first arms for a hundred years, and even then they're just adolescents.

The van rolls to a stop. The two boys in front twist around and look at me eagerly, like I'm suddenly going to put on a big show or something. Action opens the door and ushers me out to a place that's saved from being described as the middle of nowhere by very little—just the foundation to a house that was either never built or burned to the ground. There's a border of concrete with four steps leading up to a dirt lot—a rectangle filled with weeds and some bleached beer cans. It's an island of nothing in the middle of the desert, which is, as always, surprisingly green and filled with motion. Out here, without any people, everything seems strangely removed, like I'm looking through a veil. The wind reminds me of other times I've felt the wind. The sun could be on film. And all the different plants growing in the dirt. They all have names.

"Is he going to?" The driver says this as though I'm not there.

"Could you do me a favor, Miss Roberts?" Action, again, is smooth and steady, taking my hand as the wind blows his shirt tight against his torso. In other times he would have been the model for a Greek statue, a Roman foot soldier, a quarterback, the one who invented the spear. Even now I can see that he's in his element, gliding.

Nothing, for him, is veiled. "Could you go up there?" he says to me. "Would you mind please climbing up those steps now?"

The wind is blowing around scrub and trash on the little platform. Up above drift thick, white clouds.

I start climbing. These boys aren't going to hurt me. These boys are good boys. These boys will let me go.

The Ocean

I DIDN'T THINK anyone could love this lump of disrepair. I'm balding, I'm paunchy; I'm middle-aged and long hairs sprout from my knuckles. I have a gum condition that makes my breath smell like an unpleasant cheese. In the mirror I'm shocked daily to find one of those guys with a comb-over in front and a ponytail in the back. His eyes look like sad, spongy sea creatures. That's him, he's the one. It's his fault. Where's the lithe waif who used to live inside my mirrors? Where's the sprite that launched a million dollars' worth of merchandising? It sucks, I can tell you: that much I have learned. But enough self-pity. You're reading this because you want to know the secret confessions of Scott Hansen, Teen Idol, and I'm here to deliver.

Here's the truth: I was someone once. I was loved by a pink and frothy mass. I had the little girls weeping and rending their garments to paste over me. My hair, my dearly departed hair, was prized as a relic. It was biblical.

Droves of girls would make pilgrimages to my house, the studio, the town where I grew up. I'm a has-been, but I take solace in knowing that to be a has-been, you have to have been something once.

Here's a question: What is it that lives inside time? You may think it's empty, but in the space between what we are and what we once were flutter small sparrows of sorrow. There was a time in my life when I was extremely noteworthy. There was a time I was found to have evaporated. Every day I ask: Which have I really earned? The adoration or the scorn?

My fame was born when I landed the role of Jay McGuire on *The Singing Scientists.* If you've never seen the show, you must be very young. Ha ha. No really, it was about a family of mad inventors/scientists who loved all things musical. There was a kooky mom (played by Shelly Firebaum) with a Bunsen burner in the kitchen, a dad (Elrod Koil) who invented novelty gags for a living (and tried them out at home!). They had two kids, me and my onscreen sister Taffy (Kristi Shield). Taffy and me were irrepressible teen inventors with junior chemistry sets in our rooms. Taffy was always trying to invent beauty concoctions—she wore Coke-bottle glasses and was supposed to be plain—and I was forever trying to devise love potions to reel in the nubile chicks in halter tops they had back then. At the end of each show, the whole family would burst into song—usually after a successful invention, but also after a failed one. (A common theme was perseverance in light of obstacles or failure, something I've tried to take to heart in these later, more difficult years.)

As you probably know, the success of the show was phenomenal. By the fourth episode we'd attracted a huge following; by the end of the year we had the number one show in the country. The first *Singing Scientists* album went gold, and the single "Mixing It Up for You" hit number five on the charts.

The teenybopper press seized on my person almost immediately. I was featured on every cover of *Teen Boyfriend* for six months in a row. The Scott Hansen Fan Club, at its height in 1974, had over a million members. Each member had the opportunity to order a life-sized, vinyl, "kissable" poster of me, Scott Hansen. I was a human gold mine.

What did fame mean to me personally? It thrilled and frightened me. I began to have a recurring dream about a family of wolves that lived in a cupboard beneath the kitchen sink. There was a bitch and a litter of puppies curled up on one of those round, cedar-stuffed dog beds. I wish you could have heard the whimpering of those wolf pups the way I heard them in that dream. The soft yelps of baby animals—it was so soothing. In the dream, the mother grabbed me by the collar and dragged me into her den. The pups barked "hello guy!" and dogpiled me. The mama wolf began to lick my face with a warm, pink tongue that smelled of meat and olives. It was rough but pleasant. It felt like love. But then her tongue began to chafe and my face felt raw. Eventually she licked my nose off.

Right, it's only a dream, but in many ways this vision set the tone for the rest of my life. I am a man who has been damaged by love. I've been wounded and scraped and had parts of my body detached and spirited away by the hot, relentless tongue of a beast named Teenybopper. And for that I am grateful.

When I first signed on to play Jay on *The Singing Scientists*, I was an unknown kid from Modesto, California. I was an only child and my parents doted on me. Mom made meat loaf, Dad favored preknotted ties and went to work with the briefcase every morning—the whole corny routine. Only here's the strange part: my real-life dad was an inventor too. He used to come home from work and tinker around in the basement, on the moldy AstroTurf, using a broken ping-pong table as a surface for his lab experiments. He said he was "just fiddling around" with solvents and adhesives. Sometimes I'd creep down the basement stairs halfway and crouch there until the fumes overwhelmed me.

"Your father and his silly potions," my mother would say, chopping up apples for pie.

Eventually, she had to eat her words, because one of his silly potions turned out to be a new adhesive that could bond to skin without stressing "the organ," as my father came to call the human epidermis. Actually, it's the stuff on the back of the white tape used to hold down bandages. My father made a killing. We moved to Los Angeles. Almost instantly, my mother went from being a sweet, slightly ditzy housewife to a bored and bitter sophisticate. Maybe you remember Anne Bancroft in *The Graduate*? Substitute my mom. She liked animal prints, and when we went to the country club, she ordered her martinis "wet and sloppy." My father had become a superstar in his own right, a hero in the pharmaceutical industry, and he hired a secretary who knotted his tie.

My world was filled with Schwinns and indoor food courts. As it turned out, I only had a few carefree months to explore the mall scene in LA before my mother introduced me to an actors' agent at the club who signed me up and whisked me away from the real world. The agent was Tina Shinebine. *The* Tina Shinebine. She brought me to this place I am today—God bless her or curse her, I don't know which.

Does a fifteen-year-old boy know what fame means? Does he carry his responsibilities with a sense of gravity? All I knew was that I had practically unlimited access to pussy. Girls would gather outside the studio in Band-Aid-thick tube tops and rawhide sandals. Their enthusiasm was unlimited. Some of them were *really* young—we're talking twelve, thirteen. I didn't care. I had no moral mechanism. I was fifteen, weighed a hundred and twenty pounds, was as horny as a mongoose and virtually without adult supervision. When my bodyguards hustled me from my limo to the soundstage, the girls holding vigil in the parking lot would faint at the sight of me. They giggled uncontrollably. Some wet their pants.

I loved it. Those girls would do anything for me. They were like slaves.

What the wise people say is true: it *is* lonely at the top. I tried to quench the loneliness by dipping into the bottomless well of teenyboppers outside the studio gates. Here's a thought: Maybe it didn't have anything to do with loneliness. Maybe it was pure greed. So much sex. Do you know what it's like to roll around with a different teenage girl every night? A girl you've never met, who keeps your picture inside the door of her locker and has to kiss it ritually every day before she allows herself an apple and a Fresca for lunch? Do you know what it's like to forget their names, to never know their names, because they change so fast and you didn't pay any attention to what their little mouths said anyway? It was beautiful and obscene. It was like eating the most perfect, delectable chocolate over and over. Pleasure and guilt and sin and desire, and in the middle of it all was me, Scott Hansen. The girls didn't matter. I was the only one who mattered.

Which is why it's a wonder I remembered Cyndy at all. In fact, I can recall only one moment of Cyndy, and this with the aid of hypnotherapy. She was standing in front of the bathroom mirror, her back to me, naked except for a pair of white cotton panties. She was leaning forward, squeezing a pimple. When I said "what'cha doing?" she jumped and turned to face me. At that moment her face dissolves into a corona of pink light.

Who could have known all that that moment would spawn? Cyndy vanished like a puffed-out candle and in short order was replaced by an assortment of Bridgettes, Tamis, Kellys, Wandas, Tinas, Florences, Bibis, and Stephs. Then, when I got a little older and my fame was in decline, by a few Ellens, Barbis, Sukis, and Brads. And later, after *The Singing Scientists* was canceled and a pile of our records burned by an angry mob outside the Democratic National Convention; after that, when I was washed up and really drunk, there may have been a Margo, a Roxy, a Cheryl. Who knows? I was a kid. I did a volume business. It all happened fast and before the age of twenty-one. I should have been rummaging through the heavy-metal section of my local record store. I should have been buying Clearasil over the counter. Instead I had a personal assistant to do my shopping and an ocean of legs, breasts, and lips that shifted and swirled beneath my hips but never receded. I had letters and utterances and pledges of devotion; I had gifts sent by fans, including hand-knitted sweaters, hearts drawn with blood on handkerchiefs, bracelets entwined with baby teeth; but in six years there was never a distinct face in the tide, never anyone special, never a friend.

I guess it's time to talk about my sex life. My advisers tell me the best memoirs include sexual details. Okay. I can do that, though it pains me. I think I've mentioned that I'm no longer an attractive guy. My personal hygiene is lax and I'm the kind of person whose trash cans are constantly overflowing and ice trays always are empty. Anyone who can touch me now qualifies as a saint. But I'll tell you how it used to be: I liked places. If the girls were fuzzy and interchangeable, then the places were poignant and unique. I did it in hosts' closets at Hollywood parties. I did it in a pile of towels still warm from the dryer on the studio lot. I did it with a twelve-year-old in a glass elevator above the lobby of the San Francisco Hilton with my bodyguard in the car with us. I did it in Tina Shinebine's office, on her desk, next to a framed, signed eight-by-ten glossy of me, Scott Hansen, which really turned me on. I liked girls, rather than women, and I liked them pliable and pale. At my concerts, I'd have the bodyguards retrieve an assortment of leggy fawns from the audience. I wanted girls who resembled Botticelli's *Venus*, the ones with creamy complexions and stiletto limbs. When I got them alone and they were all angelic, fresh, and willing, I liked to tangle their honey-colored hair in my fist and force them to their knees. Then I'd introduce their petal-pink lips to The Monster.

Which is perhaps why I was able to retrieve even a brief memory of Cyndy in hypnotherapy—she was dark-haired, she said, with olive coloring, though she's a blonde now. She had round little hips and an articulated spine—in my guided imaging I saw the pattern of her vertebrae snaking down her back and disappearing into her white cotton briefs, which, in a deeper trance, were revealed to have had little red hearts printed on them. "Look for a girl of about thirteen years examining her complexion in the mirror," Cyndy had counseled Dr. Tofield and me.

Of course, I had taken her virginity. For this she had hitchhiked from Bakersfield to Hollywood, stolen a bicycle, and followed some sort of underground-fan-radar to my compound. There, she scaled the razor-tipped fence and calmed the dogs with a handbag full of T-bone steaks before eluding the security lights and creeping near my bedroom window. I'm not sure if I mentioned this but at the time I was the most sought-after man in the world. I commanded more money per concert and filled larger stadiums than Peter Frampton. The onslaught of uninvited girls was quite a problem for me, so I'd constructed a barrier around my wing of the house I shared with my parents. It wasn't a moat, exactly—it was more of a long, narrow reflecting pond pushed right up against the length of the house. For a while I had a baby alligator living in there as a lark, but it disappeared before the third season.

Cyndy had swum through this and thrown a rusty grappling hook secured to a line inside the rim of my windowsill, then hauled herself over. This kind of spunk and tenacity was exhibited by about two or three girls a week—girls who appeared with a thunk, soiled and panting, on my bedroom carpet. So many little girls endured so much to clamor through my window so regularly that my bodyguards used to joke that the Girl Scouts had started giving out a patch for it. Usually, I would buzz Security and have the intruder ejected; though sometimes, as seems to have been the case with Cyndy, I'd give the trooper a little treat.

Years float by and the call of the underworld deepens. Gravity pulls on the flesh, the sirens of the grave start to look pretty foxy, and I found myself taken, in these later years, by a desire to lie down on the earth in a mossy hollow and simply stir no more. Not death, exactly, but not life either, with its subtractions and aches and sticky white mysteries. "*There is as yet,*" my father wrote in his diaries, "*no adequate theory of adhesives. Perhaps the spider comprehends why the fly sticks to the web in a more profound sense than we understand the intricacies of Scotch tape healing a ripped love note.*" He was an eloquent man and I call upon his spirit now as I compose this memoir. I discovered his diary after he died of lung cancer and my mother could not be persuaded to leave the Bhagwan Shree Rajneesh for even one single week to sort out his affairs herself.

It was in the years after my father died that I began to stay in the house as much as possible. I know you've heard the rumors and many of them are true: yes, I did until recently live in my parents' house, though my parents moved out long ago. Yes, I did piss away or lose through boneheaded mismanagement the fortune I made as a teen idol (I live on a pathetic income from Pakistani residuals and travel by bus, as I have no car). Yes, I took to drink and drugs; yes, I was arrested for urinating into a fountain in a mall in Tulsa while screaming "fuck me, kill me; fuck me, kill me"—etc. It is also true that I do not know what I was doing in Tulsa or how I got there. These times have not been the best of times. Without my fame I felt unmoored. At a young age I learned that life is a performance or, worse, a publicity stunt. Imagine the emptiness of that life without an audience. Imagine the whistling canyons of abandonment.

And so, into this void, stepped Cyndy, sweet Cyndy. Cyndy of the plump arms and voluptuous hips; kind Cyndy with her eyes all rimmed in navy blue eyeliner emptying my dishwasher in a power suit. Cyndy, who saved my life and made me whole. What a great girl! As it turns out, she had been keeping an eye on me since our first encounter. Okay, maybe "stalking" is a more accurate term. She had notebooks of information, stacks of personal photographs, old telephone bills—in fact, an entire storage shed packed with my discarded mail. She began going through my trash in 1981, in the lean years, after the razor wire had gone blunt and the moat had dried up. I had no idea, of course. I just put the empty bottles out every week and retreated back inside.

Maybe you also know what it's like to stop wanting things. Maybe you too have led a worm-like existence of darkness, drink, shit, and sleep, punctuated by hazy liquor store deliveries. Maybe you've also tried to douse the painful traces of the memory that you once thrived in a rich agar of dreams and answered desires. I don't know how common this is. I still don't know much of the ways of regular folks. For a long time I was simply too famous to go out into the world without planning and protection. And after that fell away, I was too demoralized to try.

I still had some interests—drinking, if you count that, and watching TV. I also spent the last few years perfecting a method of conquering the world. One of the accountants had bought me a personal computer—I don't know exactly why. Perhaps it was so he could steal my money in a more logical, systematized manner. Anyway, I became obsessed with the computer game *The Just and the Mighty*, in which the object is to take over the world through a delicate balance of might and cunning. It takes intuition and finesse, and more than once I was reminded of my father's lab experiments (and Jay McGuire's ersatz ones). The chemistry of conquest—it consumed me! I played until my eyes swam from the glow of the screen. I played with a pounding heart. I played to win.

Eventually, I discovered a forum on the Internet where live players compete with each other for world domination. This is where I encountered Cyndy the second time, as a blinking enemy civilization mated to my computer via the phone line. I thought she was just another dictator trying to wrest control of the globe. She called her nation Rainbowland and built endless fanciful structures for the amusement of her inhabitants. I called my kingdom HansenRules!!! and built up my armies and manufacturing. She rarely won, but earned bonus points for having the happiest cities in the world. That's the kind of girl she is, sunny, filled with life and light. She began to send me friendly little messages and e-mail, punctuated by sideways smiley faces— :). At the time, I was not a happy man and did not delight in the joy of others. I have never been a partisan of the happy-face symbol and did not appreciate Cyndy's cheerful notes. Maybe you remember the bitter, misanthropic Rod Steiger in *The Pawnbroker*? Substitute me. I wanted nothing to do with smileys, and I told the dictator of Rainbowland that she could take her happy little citizens and insert them in an orifice.

Cyndy replied with this message:

"Fuck you, A-hole. I've devoted my life to you and you can't even be nice. Well fuck you. P.S. Don't fuck with me. I know exactly where you're sitting right now. I know you're wearing a green sweater. You'd better be careful, buddy."

The relief. I had a fan. I was loved.

In the years after I took her virginity, in the later part of her pubescence and on to young womanhood, Cyndy tried to contact me thousands of times. She sent letters and telegrams; she blew my bodyguards en masse; she hired a psychic. She was willing, she said, to do anything to get me back. By then I'd electrified the fence along the perimeter and was plagued by surprise nocturnal visitors no longer. I often lived in hotels anyway. My fame was like a wild dog. No one could control it. But I want to confess something: even if she had reached me, it wouldn't have made any difference. I wouldn't have remembered her, and it's doubtful I would have bothered to dally in her dark little mound again. She was not a Botticelli angel and besides, there were thousands of lost little girls who, in their loneliness, believed they had a personal relationship with me. I had a personal relationship with none of them.

For the lonely years, for the hours of fantasizing, for the money spent on merchandise bearing the name of

Scott Hansen and semen swallowed in my honor, for the acts of bravery and constant vigilance and private detectives and midnight trash runs, I just want to say, Cyndy, I'm sorry. I'm sorry I was so difficult to reach.

The first time I saw Cyndy as an adult was when I went to visit her at her condominium. Cyndy is a real estate broker and I'd like to say publicly that I'm very proud of her. She says that real estate was the natural choice for a profession, as it allowed her to drive around the LA area and monitor my well-being. She used to drive by my house two or three times a day, the market permitting. She would check for lights or movement; occasionally she'd look in my windows. I was usually drunk, she said, watching TV, masturbating, or playing a computer game. Or a combination of the above.

Anyway, I arranged a visit with Cyndy after we had become quite friendly through the computer and the phone. I hadn't been "out" in quite some time, certainly not in a social context, and my journey to her condominium was difficult and lengthy. At this period, I think I can safely say I'd touched the bottom spike in my personal graph. I'd lost the house and was living in a studio near the freeway, in a room containing a mattress, a folding chair, and a pyramid of empty vodka bottles. I'd lay awake at night, listening to the big trucks as they rolled by. Shaving—I'd given it up. On the street, people seemed compelled to comment on my appearance, like it was their duty as clean and hygienic Americans. "Take a bath!" I got, and that old standard, "Get away from me." It took me five transfers and three hours to arrive at Cyndy's complex. Someone threw a ham sandwich at me while I waited at a bus stop. Once I did arrive, it took me a half hour to figure out how to operate the security intercom.

It was with trembling fingers that I at last found myself ringing her doorbell, exhausted, panting, and terrified she wouldn't answer. What if it was all a joke? What if there wasn't anyone there? Then, with a whoosh, she threw open the door. There she was, Cyndy, in a red bathrobe slit deeply up the side, her bleached hair done up in an Ivana pouf. She had on eyeliner, perfume, lipstick, the whole arsenal. She looked pretty cute.

What happened after that is private. I know I'm supposed to tell everything here but after all she is my lawfully wedded wife and keeps me on a pretty short leash—ha ha. I'm not sure if I should even put that in. I realize there are a lot of rough edges in this memoir and I trust my ghostwriter, Stacey Richter, to clean them up. But let me just mention this: ravishing as Cyndy looked, what took my breath away was her knack for interior decoration. Scott Hansen posters, some framed, lined the walls. A few were peppered with lipstick smacks. Others seemed to have been tenderized with a blunt instrument, maybe a fork. Everywhere I turned I saw myself, young and groomed, staring dreamily into my own eyes. In the corner was a Scott Hansen shrine, ringed with candles. The centerpiece was the life-size "kissable" fan club poster. It didn't look so good. The edges had been perforated to lace, probably from being tacked up and taken down so many times. It was puckered, like it had been wetted, though just in parts.

"Hi, Scott," Cyndy said, with that bright smile I've come to know so well. "Thank God you finally changed your shirt."

• • •

The time comes, for every lonely player, when he stops trying to win the game and begins to plot his own demise. Solitaire fans know what I mean—how you reach a moment when the cards turn against you and instead of struggling for victory, something clicks, and you start to wallow in your own defeat. It was like this for me with *The Just and the Mighty*. I began to starve my own citizens. I lobbed nuclear missiles into the atmosphere for the fun of it. I caused global warming, drought, pollution, and unrest. I changed my government from democratic to despotic and watched production plummet. My citizens revolted and perished by fire. The polar ice caps melted and farmland turned to swamp. I wanted to see how low I could go. I wanted to roll in the odor of bad things.

Cyndy, too, was no stranger to the dark side. She had grown accustomed to unrequited love, she said, and even when I was washed up and she knew she could ring my doorbell anytime, naked and tied with a big, pink bow, she couldn't bring herself to do it. Her life was woven from hunger and need, and she'd begun to despise me for the grip I had on her. She bought a gun. She'd drive up to my house and stare through the windows at me, sitting in front of the computer—*playing that fucking game,* she said. Even when I was fat, ugly, and drunk, her yearning for me would make her sick to her stomach. She'd stand outside my window, the heels of her pumps sinking into the damp soil, and after a while she'd bring the gun to the glass and direct it at my head. She claimed she spent two afternoons a week at the practice range. Every night she was doing forty, fifty push-ups—a lot for a woman. Maybe you remember Robert De Niro in *Taxi Driver*? A half dozen times, she said, she pointed the gun at my head; and each time she turned it away and brought it to her own temple. When she tells me this I always think: the dirt swallowing her heels came from the same plot of earth as the dirt that was smeared across her face the night she'd swum the moat to get into my room. What happened to the pluck and spirit of that little dark-haired girl? What sparrows of sorrow had made her turn all that wild energy against herself?

Here's a thought: Maybe a has-been is a wonderful thing to be. Maybe to have and to lose is infinitely richer than never to have at all. Perhaps I'm a wise person. I'm not sure. I still haven't seen much of the world. But I do know this: Cyndy hates me. Cyndy hates me and I'm glad. With every cry of "fat slob," "lazy asshole," and "useless jerk-off" that trips from her lips, I feel her bloom a little. With every dollar she pilfers from the dregs of my empire, I feel her come a little more into her own. What is love, if not a form of punishment? Ever since Cyndy was ten years old, she said she knew I was the man for her. Cyndy's mother used to ask why she slept all scrunched up against the wall and she replied, "I have to leave room on the other side for Scott Hansen." Well, she doesn't have to leave room anymore. If she wants to sell all my belongings to the highest bidder or, if that fails, to curio collectors at swap meets and craft fairs, I understand. I had my time in the light, and now she wants hers.

If this sounds noble, it's not. Love for me has never been a decoration—it's what my life is made of, the primordial fluid. Isn't hate a form of love? Isn't adoration a form of panic? Isn't my devotion to Cyndy a kind of atonement? What do I know? I learned about human relationships at the hands of children. Those little girls, I'll tell you this about them: they may be young, but they're fierce. Love to them is everything, a total obsession. They're brief, hot little lights, and even when they change their minds, you can bet they really meant it once, with every cell and drop of liquid in their pink-scented bodies.

When I sit, now, at the helm of our camper—perhaps the last solid representation of capital I have—and think about my life, I envision brightly colored bodies of water, like the blue parts of the map in *The Just and the Mighty*. At first I was a child with a little pond of love—the love of my parents—to sustain me, nestled between grasses and valleys and hills. Then I was swept up by a powerful ocean—strawberry-scented, with crests of lip gloss, yes, but an ocean still. How many people ever plunge into a sea of love? How many of us are worshiped as gods? I really had it once. Me and the missus may appear to be a middle-aged fart and his hectoring wife schlepping between flea markets on the backroads of the nation in an old Sir Wind-a-Long camper, selling vintage Scott Hansen paraphernalia (autographed), but we've sipped divine nectar. I was a god and she, my acolyte. Now I'm paying, but isn't there justice in that? My ocean dried up, but I've discovered that all I really need is a single drop to conjure up the whole—Cyndy, whose name I'll never forget again, whose name I say over and over in my head when she deigns to perform her wifely duty—a shipwrecked lover from an ocean of love, Cyndy mine.

Rats Eat Cats

I HAVE ALWAYS wanted to be a Cat Lady. A Cat Lady is an old woman who lives "by herself" with as many as seventy-five cats in a one-bedroom apartment. In life, she shuns human company, and when she dies, no one realizes until the neighbors are overwhelmed by the fumes of her decomposing body, which is generally discovered half decayed and partially eaten by her pets—pets who really, really loved her in life but can't survive without their cat chow unless they're a little scrappy when faced with such adversity. Plucky. Resourceful.

That's what they said the Prozac would do for me: make me plucky and resourceful. And it has! Before, I never would have imagined I could sustain twenty-one kitties in my studio apartment. I wouldn't have even tried; end of discussion. Then I'd go sob in front of the mirror and squeeze zits. But now—it's as though the cobwebs have been vacuumed from my brain. I realize anything is possible. I can live my dreams. I'm a beautiful young woman with lots of potential who can have as many pets as she wants! Life is exciting, and shiny.

Currently, most of my art already revolves around cats and cat products. *Feline Flambé*, accepted for display in the Young Artists of SF show at The Lab, was a lifesize lapcat made entirely of fur harvested from my personal kitties, formed around a core of chicken wire. The enclosed slides show *Feline Flambé* as it appeared on display, and also during the performance portion of the show, when I doused the piece in lighter fluid, then torched it. This was meant to symbolize the destruction of affection via the flames of betrayal. Most of my plastic art is about the fragility, perishability, and combustibility of love. Basically, I believe that love and betrayal are very, very closely linked and that everybody gets screwed over in the end, or eaten by their cats, or turned over to the cops; or worse, become cops themselves. Or they just give up and become their parents. I believe that most contemporary art is about the fear of "becoming" one's parents. I would include my own work within this category.

The grant, should I receive it, would therefore be used to fund the main project of my artistic career, which I call the Cat Lady Project. I intend to nurture this persona of "Cat Lady" over the years, until I am truly, to the core, an old lady who lives in a one-bedroom apartment with seventy-five cats. The most important part of the project, then, would commence when I reached an age wherein I would be considered "old," in, say, forty-some years. At that time, I would be living in a small apartment in a densely populated city. I would constantly wear the same sweater, and maybe a synthetic wig. I'd have several litter boxes in my apartment, and this litter would be changed infrequently. I would receive either welfare or social security, and spend most (if not all) of these public moneys on cat food. As part of the project, I'd rarely leave my home, and when I did, I'd mutter to myself. Cat hair would be embedded in my sweater. It would almost appear that my sweater was *made* of cat hair. I would be unlike anyone working in the art world. My piece could not be commodified (sold) or destroyed, at least not while I'm alive. I believe I'd be quite content.

I know that when you add up the factors—the twenty-one cats, the cat hair sculpture, the Prozac, etc., you may mistakenly think I'm well on the way to becoming a Cat Lady without financial support from the National Endowment for the Arts. But I think we can all agree that Cat Ladies don't just "happen." They have to be nurtured, and this is an especially crucial time in the development of this project because of the possibility of derailment by the Rat Boy. In the event that you are unfamiliar with the term, "Rat Boys" are young psychotics who raise rats and have no friends aside from rodents. Rat Boys frequently live in one-bedroom apartments filled with the plastic tubing and glass aquariums of homemade rodent warrens. They are lonely, pathetic beings who, like Cat Ladies, assauge their solitude with the company of small, furry creatures. But unlike Cat Ladies, Rat Boys nurture violent fantasies of destruction and triumph. They are basically like evil geniuses in comic books: they want to rule the world, and if they can't do that, they'll destroy it trying.

Dearest Granting Committee, there is a Rat Boy living above me in my apartment building, and I believe he has declared me his mortal enemy! His sole purpose in life is to "bust a cap" into my pet kitties. He would, in essence, like to freeze the whole Cat Lady Project in its tracks. He believes that his rats and my kitties cannot live in the same building. He has personally told me that cats are "antirats," and that when the two come into contact, one of them must be destroyed, and that a small but potent particle of matter (energy) is emitted in the process. This Rat Boy has a very strong odor of cedar chips about him, and I would swear on a stack of Bibles that he's never brushed his hair since I've moved in here. Whenever I see him he's wearing the same sweatshirt that says "Dribble" on it, and no one knows why it says "Dribble."

The Rat Boy pesters me every day. He says there will be no peace until either the cats or the rats go. Then he tightens an imaginary noose around his neck and makes a noise in his throat like he has a hairball. I would be the first to agree that sure, there have been problems, but if Rat Boy could keep his huffing little rodents *inside* their cages everything would be fine. Yes, okay, Roach-Muffin did find an adolescent rat in the kitchen cupboard and dragged it out onto the linoleum. Yes, Roach-Muffin did administer the killing bite to the back of the rat's neck while my other kitties looked on eagerly, practically taking notes (cats are very intelligent, but they need to be taught the "killing bite"). But it isn't my fault that Rat Boy's rats are running up and down the pipes between our apartments! I would be happy to find a solution to this conflict. More than happy.

I have made definite efforts to this end. The Rat Boy did accept my invitation to come over to negotiate a truce. Most of my kitties slunk into the corners or adopted a distant, glassy look when he entered. At first the Rat Boy stomped around, saying "darn cats, darn cats." But after a while he calmed down, and then the Boy told me, with moist eyes, that he loves his rats very dearly. He feels he has to release them from their cages fairly often so they can run around on his "Dribble" sweatshirt so that he can be close to them, and not feel so lonely. He said sometimes he lets a bunch out at once, and has races and other organized group activities, which he referred to as "maneuvers." (I believe that he is hoping to train these rats into a ravenous "rat army" that will respond to the Rat Boy's evil bidding.) Sometimes, he informed me, a rat will escape and go hide in the drapes or something, then crawl down the pipes to my apartment. He told me this like he was "proving" how intelligent his rats are. I said—Oh yeah, like sometimes "a" rat gets loose, like one single rat!

He said, Okay. Maybe more than one.

We were snacking from a platter of assorted lunch meats with a parsley garnish, a very old-lady kind of food presentation. Even at this early age I am trying to emulate old women. I believe girls have much to learn from grannies: how to dress with dignity, how to be self-sufficient, how to live simply and frugally, and how to enjoy solitude, to name but a few. I can't wait to be old. Then everything will be finished, decided, and I won't have to slog through life anymore making decisions that affect me. I won't have to figure out what or who to "be," because I will have already been. I can tell quaint, charming stories of the gentlemen who courted me, or what a beautiful dress I wore to a big rave (that term will sound folksy by then), but I won't have to participate in all the upsetting fear, uncertainty, and pain that comes with youth.

Then, as I am sitting with the Rat Boy, offering him my finest geriatric platter of processed luncheon meats and limp Ritz crackers, a wet, glossy rat pokes its head out from under the sink.

"Oh my God!" said the Rat Boy. "It's Ratsputin!"

For the life of me, I don't know how he tells those creatures apart. However, I decided to hold my tongue and mind my manners. When Kleptomaniac pounced, I was demurely pouring the Rat Boy another cup of tea.

Kleptomaniac is a fluffy, temperamental flirt with a black coat and white socks. When I come home, she flings herself onto her back and rolls around on the carpet like she's auditioning to be an "exotic dancer." She also has a penchant for stealing and hoarding the few available cat toys in the apartment, hence the name. She's a Zsa Zsa of a cat, so naturally I couldn't have been more surprised to see her leap from the kitchen counter onto the neck of Ratsputin like a lioness taking down an antelope. The rat squealed and bucked a few times, panted, then went soft. A puff of fur (whose?) descended through the air. It happened very quickly.

Rat Boy became extremely agitated. He grabbed a broom and tried to knock Kleptomaniac off his rodent, but it was too late. By the time he drove her off and picked up Ratsputin by the tail, the little guy was completely deceased. His head flopped around on his neck like a puppet.

Heavens to Betsy, I think I said.

Of course he was upset, but what was I supposed to do? Cats eat rats—everybody learns that in high school biology. Rat Boy stood by the sink weeping softly while he wound Ratsputin in a clean paper towel. A blot of blood seeped through the shroud. I felt like I was watching my hopes for a truce being obliterated beneath the spreading stain.

"Murderer," he muttered at Kleptomaniac, sucking a lump of snot back into his nose. She seemed unperturbed, and licked her paws with gusto.

I gently suggested that if he didn't want my cats to kill his rats, then perhaps he should keep his rats confined to his apartment.

"Cat-kisser," he moaned, cradling the rat's body close to his chest. "You're a dirty cat-kisser." He sort of curled up there by the kitchen sink, moaning, with his face very red. "He's still warm," he choked, holding the back of his hand to the little bundle in the paper towel. I hate to say it, but it looked like a burrito. A rat burrito. I extended my hand, trying to touch him on the shoulder.

"Get away," he yelled. He said some other things that weren't very nice too, but mostly he kept calling me a "cat-kisser" in this tone that made it sound like he was calling me a Klansman. I said I was sorry, but it seemed like he didn't hear me. Finally I asked him to kindly leave my apartment, which he did while muttering, "It's you or me, baby, you or me," so you can see why I'm upset. This boy is sociopathic—it is the nature of Rat Boys to be unbalanced but this one is severe. I've seen how weird he can be, and he is making threats. I feel it is essential that I move into a new apartment building, where I can pursue my goal of becoming a Cat Lady in safety and quiet. Cat Ladies do not like conflict. Cat Ladies do not appreciate events. They like to sit quietly in front of the radio and knit while their kitties bat at a ball of yarn. The whole project of commerce or romance or even amusement is no longer an issue for the Cat Lady. Cat Ladies are closed systems.

Therefore, it is imperative that I receive a grant so I can move out of my apartment! Moving is expensive, and I don't have enough cash right now to do it, and it's doubtful I'm going to get a raise at the library where I toil at the very schoolmarmish task of shelving books. You see, I'm serious about this project! In every part of my life I'm yearning for my golden years. I realize this may sound "way out" to some of you people on the committee, but I know that others among you have funded projects involving the spiritual properties of body fluids and enactments of outsider performance and artistic concepts employing biting social satire—Cat Lady is all these things! And more! Plus, it is completely not indecent. Cat Ladies are the *definition* of decency—meek, old-fashioned, disapproving. When a kid spits on the sidewalk (who cares if he calls himself an artist?), Cat Lady mutters "shame on you."

What could possibly be more worthy of public funding?

Dearest Granting Committee, I hope to finish this quickly, lest the entire Cat Lady Project become jeopardized by the fact that I no longer have any cats. Today I came home from work and somebody (I think we know who) had chucked a brick through my window. There were cats on the ledge. My kitties are indoor kitties, and I don't think they know much about heights and calculating risks and landing on their feet. I live on the fourth floor but there's a negotiable fire escape, and upon counting my pets I've found that two of them, Lopsock and Flexible, are gone. Feared dead. Leapt into air and landed on concrete? Flattened by a bus?

I more than suspect the Rat Boy. Tacked to my door, I found a note that said "Rats Eat Cats," and then he had drawn a picture of a muscle-bound rat decapitating a kitten. When I realized I'd lost two of my darlings, I felt very old—tired and resigned, like nothing could ever fill in that missing space. Then I sat on the stoop and thought about how the Cat Lady Project is also about a kind of vacancy, a sort of perpetually windswept room that needs to be filled up with small, velvety creatures who can always be replaced, because without their warmth and purring and nonjudgmental love reflex, the emptiness would overwhelm a girl. Or whatever, a Cat Lady.

I was sitting on the stoop, muttering, "Oh my, oh my," weeping, with a saucerful of wet food, hoping my lost kitties could be enticed home, when the Rat Boy approached on the sidewalk and sat down beside me. He held a waxed carton of milk and I remember I thought that didn't seem like a rat beverage. He and I sat there looking straight ahead into the traffic passing on Valencia, at the bums and crack ladies of the evening on the sidewalk, because we don't live in a very nice neighborhood and the projects are across the street. One Christmas, I found an intact turkey, golden brown and still in its foil roasting pan, that somebody had flung into the yard around the projects. It was like the last line to a story illustrating the sorrow and hate people put each other through during holidays. Thankfully, Cat Ladies are exempt from these problems.

"Hey," Rat Boy said. I was crying harder and he put

his hand on my hair, very softly, and rubbed me there like I was a pet.

"You!" I said, and then I couldn't really say anything.

"What is it?" His voice cracked, like he was crying himself. Then I looked over and his face was red and scrunched up like he actually was almost crying. I guess Rat Boy is very sensitive.

"You know," I accused him.

"I don't," he protested, but I knew he was lying. He was the one who declared the cat/rat war. Rat Boys by their nature are predators who feed on conflict.

All I could do though was cry harder, because not only was Rat Boy an evil schemer, he was a liar too. Which was like twisting a knife, that a boy drinking milk and touching my hair gently was a liar. He put his arm around my shoulder and I sat there for a minute not knowing if I hated him or what. I decided I did and squirmed out from under his elbow and ran inside.

When I got in I taped up the hole in the window. The kitties are still missing. The Rat Boy hasn't stopped by or called.

Now things are even worse. I am afraid the Cat Lady Project is in mortal danger. Though one positive thing happened and that is that Lopsock and Flexible came home. Yesterday I found them mewing beneath my taped-up window, looking trashed and sort of guilty. Lopsock had a wild, harassed gleam in her eye, like she had been up snorting coke all night, and liked it. She also had a spot of oil on her coat—a dark, rat-like spot—I guess she'd been crouching under a car. That would be just like Lopsock, who loves to crawl underneath things. Flexible was also not in such tiptop shape, I'm sad to report. He was dragging a back leg and was damp and looked just miserable, like an old man waiting at a bus stop in the rain. The little guy needed a trip to the vet, a considerable drain on my finances, but what else could I do? They trust me. I put Flexible into a laundry basket with some towels and began the trek to the vet.

On the way out of the building I ran into Rat Boy. Rat Boy seemed very concerned about Flexible, if you can believe that. "Poor little murderer," he said, and stroked his head. I was shocked that Flexible let himself be touched by Rat Boy—but he pushed his nose into his hand and broke into a purr. Over my polite protests, Rat Boy insisted on accompanying me to the vet's office. He insisted on carrying the basket with Flexible in it too, and though I wasn't sure this was right, I'm an old-fashioned girl and felt obliged to let him. While we walked, I looked Rat Boy over. He had combed his hair, and his "Dribble" sweatshirt looked freshly laundered.

It was a sunny day, and Flexible managed to lift his head over the edge of the basket to watch the city float by. Everything looked especially bright, even the dirt on the sidewalk and the grime on the buses. I had a funny feeling about the Rat Boy then. It made me afraid to look at him. It was like there was some sort of string connecting us. I listened to the sound of his shoes hitting the sidewalk. I fell behind several paces so I could look at him carrying my kitty. I thought he looked cute.

At the vet's, we waited on a couch beside a potted palm that smelled of dog urine. There were a few other owners sitting there with their pets straining on leashes or shivering on their laps. Rat Boy told me that he liked my sweater. For a while he seemed to be staring into the dying palm. Then, in a faltering voice, he told me that when he had found me on the stoop the day before, holding the bowl of wet food and crying, he decided he never wanted to see me looking so sad again. He said it broke his heart. Then he leaned in close to stroke Flexible. I could smell the scent of cedar clinging to him.

Dearest Granting Committee, it's a well-known fact that both Cat Ladies and Rat Boys find personal contact repugnant. It is part of a Cat Lady's nature to detest being touched. That's why I'm terrified for the fate of the Project! Because when we got back to our apartment building, Rat Boy saw me to my door, but before I could get inside he leaned over and kissed me. On the lips, lightly, I could feel the softness of his mouth and the warmth of his breath—and when I just stood there and said "Oh my," he kissed me again, this time letting his tongue dip into the inside of my lower lip, just barely. I was immobilized, pierced, like he had administered the killing bite.

Boys kiss girls, everyone learns that in high school biology, but I'm not sure that Rat Boys can, in good faith, kiss Cat Ladies. I'm worried that my entire Project may be in jeopardy, and I'm frightened. Obviously, I can't pursue a life of lonely eccentricity effectively if I am kissing the Rat Boy. But I found it difficult to stop. I invited the Rat Boy inside and he lay down next to me on the couch. We made out while my kitties crawled all over us, purring and kneading our soft parts while the Rat Boy said "You vicious murderess" and kissed Sir Cat-a-lot on the nose. Then he told me I was his adorable evil nemesis and bit my earlobe and began unbuttoning my blouse. I tried to frame this as an experience from my youth that I could recount in a crotchety manner once I had safely become a crone, but the Rat Boy smelled so foresty and was tracing circles on my belly with such rapt captivation that I forgot about being retired and abandoned myself to the pure zing of the moment. Then Rat Boy started murmuring in my ear about opposites colliding and sparking love energy or something—it was kind of pornographic, but I liked it. To be honest, Dearest Granting Committee, I liked it all.

Later, Rat Boy staple-gunned a piece of screening over the hole behind my sink so that if a rat gets loose, it will just shimmy on down to the next apartment, where the Snake Couple live. I have to admit I was glad to have him there with me. Every time I looked at him, I wanted to slide my hands underneath the "Dribble" sweatshirt. Every time I heard his voice, it was like stepping into a warm bath.

But I'm worried he might be dissolving something inside me that's very precious, very dear! He might be clogging up my urge to transform my life into a solitary artwork. I'm afraid he could possibly undermine the entire Cat Lady Project, and that the desire to give it up is already crouching within me. With a little prompting, I'm afraid I'd relinquish my work, and marry the Rat Boy, and move to the suburbs and become occupied with a plot of lawn and a baby or two. The years would trot by, and when I had the time or the itch to take up art again it would probably be a craft: cross-stitching or needlepoint, something practical. Because by the time I reached that advanced point in my life, I wouldn't be able to imagine making things for beauty or meaning or relief. I'd crochet coverlets that fit the arms of my chairs exactly. I'd make extra, and sell them at church bazaars, and somewhere in the little warrens of my mind there'd be a memory of having once been a wild, bohemian artist; of inventing myself and living very close to the flutter of my fears and desires. And then, I'd say to my kids: I met your father and gave it all up. We both did. He was a Rat Boy. I was a Cat Lady. We canceled each other out.

Rat Boy insists it doesn't have to be like this. He says we can collaborate and that it would in fact be pretty cool; that conflict is an exciting part of being human creatures. He says love and art aren't mutually exclusive. He wants to use some of the grant money to raise a baby rat and a newborn kitten in the same cage. He believes they'll grow up to be companions, and that eventually we may be able to have an entire apartment full of cats and rats who play and live together in peace and harmony. The cats will forget the killing bite and groom the rats with their sandpaper tongues. The rats will sleep curled in the cats' paws and poke their noses into their ears. He says it's been done once before, in India.

Rules for Being Human

IT'S A BOOZY night, and the regulars are practically dry-humping the bar—broken specimens convinced as usual they're engaged in something called *fun*. In life I was one of them, a sauced and angry son of a bitch. Pissed on. Forced to eviscerate cockroaches with my naked soles. Now I'm at peace, sort of, with all the other cats sort of at peace in this sticky barroom, not thoroughly mopped once in thirty-four years. Ghosts drink free here, and the place is infested with them. For the most part regulars, whole ones: a pair of coeds mashed in a car crash, pulpy but intact, dripping polyps of flesh onto the floor. Same shredded party dresses all these years. A husband carrying his wife's bullet in his heart, leaking fluid from the wound. Gup Gup, a pale, bloated accountant dead of liver rot. An assortment of translucent extras. The night is yet young. I start with a wound like a ham steak at mid-thigh and end in a pair of blood-soaked engineer boots, severed when my body slipped trying to hop a boxcar. Misjudged.

Three sheets. The arms grabbed a ladder, the body wrenched sideways, and the legs jackknifed under the wheels where I was liberated from the old trunk faster than you can slice the tip off a carrot. I lay twitching on the tracks while the head, torso, and other leg floated off toward El Paso.

That was 1964. I don't know how these things get divided up. I don't know where the soul-a-ma-gig went. Maybe I've got it and the rest of my body is an emptied-out husk. Or maybe I'm just some freakish receptacle of consciousness—the sentient severed limb. Other body parts have been known to scramble in here: a hacked-off hand, a couple of unaffiliated fingers. I avoid 'em. They're like dogs. Full of impulse but with no real intelligence. The hand trembles and raises a drink, over and over. The fingers scratch or tamp cigarettes. The same thing, over and over. Ghosts are obsessive-compulsive. Me, I like to hop over to the jukebox and kick the shit out of it whenever that Hall and Oates song comes on—"You Make Me Feel Brand New." I don't even think about it anymore. It's Pavlovian.

The living coexist with the dead pretty smoothly around here. Yeah, we play our little tricks. The hinges on the bathroom doors have an unnatural squeak, but a tipsy audience misses the nuances. Tonight the place is packed; I've seen some of these faces almost every night for the last twenty-some years, but no moralizing, okay? *I* don't know what a person needs to get through the night, or a life: an amber liquid, a bottle of pills, an anonymous roll in the hay. All I know is what it's like to be compelled. It's like I have to be here. I'm waiting for something.

In the meantime I watch, and when I feel like it, I kick

some ankle under the table. I roll in spills to get the smell of liquor on me. I avoid the loose fingers and the sorority skirts. Ghosts don't like to talk to other ghosts. Ghosts are creepy. I don't like most of the corporeal patrons either. You'd think we'd be nuzzling up to the most lively specimens—the loudest talkers, the most audacious flirts, trying to suck up a little of that energy. No such spirit. We're just looking for the living who remind us of ourselves. We want to touch the sore spot. We're ghosts. By definition we want to do it again.

When I can, I hang with one particular cat with stringy black hair and an armful of tattoos who goes by the name of Vlad. The first time I saw him in here he was nine years old, gripping his mother's hand. She set him up with a Rob Roy and a handful of quarters for the pinball machine, then proceeded to work her way through a half dozen jiggers of the very cheapest scotch. Vlad, back then, was known as Johnny. *I* even remember how when he finished with the quarters he stood by his mother's stool, tugging on her skirt while she let some character above paw her. From where we stood, you could see his tongue going in and out of her head.

He and I were about the same height then. Now he's a tall motherfucker with long, thin legs he likes to keep wrapped in the tightest of black jeans. They're like stems. I can't get enough of those bad boys; I kick 'em constantly. Gets him into fights but he's calmed down a bit now that he's in his thirties. Once an addict, now just a drunk.

Certain lost and pained young girls who pass the evening in taverns topple for Vlad; he's needy but plays it tough. They can see the hurt, vulnerable boy beneath the bluster. Women his own age won't have anything to do with him. The calcified edges that don't let anything in will eventually encase him—a lonely old boozer. A fate I was more or less divorced from. But for now he still radiates a romantic picture of himself that includes certain heroic deeds of misadventure and danger—driving all night hopped up on pills, playing the trumpet at 2 A.M., jumping a boxcar. I can't stay away from him. He has that promise for me, of wholeness.

This despite his knack for making spectacularly stupid pronouncements: "Pink is not a shade of red"; "No girl has ever faked it with me"; "Vegetables give you cancer"; "Cigarettes improve your endurance." This evening Vlad is wearing black suede boots, circa 1989. A very pointy toe. He's sitting with the verbs, Pat and Bob. Whenever I see Bob, his soft, fat body and his little German eyeglasses, I think of the joke: what do you call a fellow with no arms and no legs floating in a swimming pool? It replays in my head like a tired jukebox selection. These three boys are reformed honor students who've gotten stuck with their thug acts. It's like when a mother tells her kid not to roll his eyes back into his head or they'll stay that way. I went to Vlad's bar mitzvah. Bob was a National Merit Scholar in high school. Pat was an altar boy. Now they're manual laborers who wear black clothes at night and complain about not getting what they never tried to have.

Pat runs his fingers through a puddle of beer on the table. He has a narrow, goat-like head that doesn't quite fit his muscular body. A hopefulness in his face that you often see in the living in the early hours of the night. He's the dumbest of the three. Workingman. Ladies' man. Wearing Doc Martens, black with yellow stitching, very nice.

"What the fuck is that?" inquires Pat.

A baby is crying. In the center of the barroom the dead coeds are hanging all over a girl carrying an infant. The girl has dark circles under her eyes that take over her face. She balances the baby carrier on her hip like a bag of groceries.

"That's a human infant," Vlad explains.

"It would seem that you were one," Bob elaborates, "once."

The coeds coo and make kissy face over the bundle of pink. These two generally function in unison, like a pair of animatronic elves repeating some joyless task on a Christmas display. They pass a ghost cigarette through the baby's body, then throw back their heads and cackle. The mother looks distracted and a little confused, as if she could sense the violation. The girls maneuver the cigarette so that ghost smoke crawls out of the kid's mouth. The living don't see this. Only ghosts get to see it, but I'm sure it would give all of us a chuckle. Forcing dogs to smoke, making babies smoke—dead or alive, drunks all have the same sense of humor.

"Look." It's the mother. She's tucked herself into the empty seat beside Vlad. She gazes at him with sad eyes. The baby, in its little carrier, goes on the table next to the pitcher of beer. She speaks in a high, little-girl voice. "It's not mine. It's my sister's. This is mine." She hefts an enormous handbag into the air. "I've got it all."

"Give me some," suggests Pat.

"Har de har," she snaps.

The girl is wearing leather sandals that reek of foot and patchouli oil. I would guess she's never had a pedicure. Up above the boys are gawking at the infant. Vlad dips a finger in his beer and touches it to the baby's lips.

The kid wrinkles his nose and clutches his little fingers around a knot of empty air.

"Are you sure you should do that?" Pat asks.

"Infants are immune to alcohol," Vlad explains.

"Hey!" the girl protests, taking note of Vlad's shenanigans. But her voice has a flirtatious ring. Then she pops up and heads toward the bar.

I can hear her whining to the bartender: "Okay. Okay. I just came in to make a phone call. . . ."

The boys continue to stare at the baby as though it were some high-tech electronic device.

"I'm not going to touch it," Pat says.

She returns with a tumbler full of whiskey. "What do you have to do around here?" She runs her tongue around the lip of the glass.

"I'm going to break into the zoo and set the animals free," replies Vlad.

"Oh yeah," she says, "I understand. I'm a vegetarian." She dips into her handbag and pulls out a Slim Jim. "This," she says, "is from before."

It goes on the table next to the kid. Vlad lights a cigarette and unbends a knee. I envy those gams, long and sinewy and connected by veins and arteries to a pumping heart. I rock his boot gently.

"They say it's all humane and shit, but there isn't a creature alive that wants to spend its existence caged."

"I could survive. I have everything I need in here." She pats her purse.

"Fuck. You couldn't get me in a cage. They've tried."

Pat and Bob just watch Vlad when he's with the ladies—they can't compete. He's the one. I can see their brains chugging, trying to figure out what he's got.

The baby jerks its arms and legs like an upturned bug. "Huh!" it says. Bob touches it on the nose, then rolls his eyes.

"Every little thing." The girl starts removing items from the purse: keys, tampons, Band-Aids, breath mints, pills.

On the wall above the table, a hand crouches in a plastic floral arrangement. It's invisible to my friends in the booth, but they probably wouldn't notice anyway. Something on the table has attracted it. It's making a clutching motion, over and over—hungry, the way we get. Personally, I'm praying that Vlad and the girl will start playing footsie.

Vlad takes the tampon and pretends to put it up his nose.

"Don't be a moron," Bob warns. "It'll get stuck and we'll have to take you to the emergency room and explain."

"Explain what?" Vlad dangles the tampon string over the baby's head. It starts to cry. "These things work great for gunshot wounds."

"Now," says the mother. She picks up her empty glass and weaves over to the bar.

"How do we make it stop?" asks Pat.

"Insert something into its air passages," suggests Vlad.

"Give it a cigarette," adds Pat, letting one dangle from his mouth à la the dangerous.

The hand floats down the wall with its fingers curling and reaching. When I see its pasty fist closing around the girl's rabbit foot key chain, bright, yellow, and fluffy, I realize I want it too. Very badly.

Vlad watches the rabbit foot levitate above the tabletop

with a disinterested expression, like he's used to this old conjuring trick. "I think there's something funny about this baby."

The kid is drowsing in its little plastic case, baby-shaped the way a violin case is violin-shaped. Every now and then it opens its eyes and focuses on some phantom spot above the table. It could be that we are in the presence of ghosts even ghosts can't see. It burps weakly. It opens its mouth like a landed fish. The mother is nowhere to be seen. This infant doesn't seem so hardy. I am wondering what happens if it dies. Am I going to have to hop over a slobbering baby for eternity? Or until, God help me, the bar finally closes its doors for good?

I try not to think about unpleasant things. I try to pretend I'm drunk. Someone has slugged a quarter in the jukebox and selected the Patti Smith song I so dig. It's an epic rock song about a punk kid's dying moment, a brief peak of vitality that spikes up while his lifeblood drains onto the tiled hallway. It's the only song on that jukebox I can still stand. As he's bleeding out his last, the kid has a vision of running horses, a sexy, rhythmic mirage. It reminds me of my train. Pain, and then a last spurt of life.

I decide to work on swiping the rabbit foot from the disembodied hand. It's scampered off, dodging legs across the damp and coated linoleum. The floor is *my* arena! The thing darts between a pair of black pumps, through a forest of ankles, prancing like a Chihuahua with a slipper in its mouth. I step on some toes and corral it into a corner.

The coeds join in, bending over the hand and chanting dramatically, "Go *into* the light, go *into* the light." Then they fall all over themselves giggling hysterically. Once a man drove his pickup up a pole outside the bar. We all crowded into the doorway and watched him floating above the damage. He was middle-aged, Mexican, in cowboy boots. There were magnetized saints all over the cab of the truck. I wanted to sing to him, something, I didn't know what. That was before that song about the dying boy turned up on the jukebox. I would have sung that.

As it turned out, I didn't sing anything. A hot pink tunnel erupted in the air next to the crumpled front end, spilling the fine brightness of the heavens across the shattered glass.

"Wait!" screamed the coeds, tears streaming down their faces. "Don't!"

I'd never seen them so excited. You can bet *we* all shrank from the light. We retreated inside our barroom quick. You won't see us bowing to acceptance. You won't see us going gentle into one of those gaping pink things.

The hand trembles in the corner, pinching the rabbit foot. It's a left hand. Probably hacked off by the right.

"Pretty, pretty, pretty," the girls murmur, bending over charmingly. Their dresses are shredded here and there. Inside their wounds are fuzzy, like something glimpsed through a window screen.

The hand seems to hear them. It rocks back on its stump and relaxes a little. It tilts upward like it's hoping for a treat. Sensing opportunity, I kick. The rabbit's foot takes flight and lands at the toe of a patron, who picks it up and puts it in his pocket.

"Lucky day," he says.

The living get everything I want.

• • •

I duck into the ladies' room to scan for fresh reading material. The place is dirty and pink and has the fruity stink of industrial cleaning fluid. Nothing new has appeared, as usual, so I peruse the inside door of the left-hand stall. I always read this part. In bubbling, teenage script:

Rules for Being Human!

1. *There are no mistakes in life, only lessons!*
2. *The learning never stops!*

There's more, but it's obscured by a snarl of black pen offering the advice: *If you* bitches *could stay sober for one weekend, you might get a fucking life.*

I'm always cheered to find I'm not the only one without a life.

I hop back to Vlad and lean against his dusty pants leg. He and Bob are playing with the baby. The mother has not returned. Vlad has a shot glass of bourbon in front of him and he's dribbling it down a straw into the baby's sea anemone mouth.

"Yeeeee!" the baby says.

"I don't think it's into it," Vlad observes.

"You're such a fuckhead," Bob drones in his fat-boy monotone. "You're supposed to give it milk. Don't you know anything about caring for your own species?"

"Why don't *you* do it?"

"I don't want to get involved."

"Hey, sweetheart." Vlad waves a girl over. They come right to him. "Get me a glass of milk, will you?"

"Holy shit," she says, coming closer, "what *is* that?" She touches its velvet forehead.

"Don't touch! This isn't a petting zoo!"

She looks offended, but softens when Vlad picks up the infant and cradles it in his arms.

"That is so cute," she beams.

Bob is pouting. "Babies obviously get chicks."

She gets him a glass of milk. Vlad mixes a little whiskey in and dribbles it down a straw. The baby coos softly and waves its arms. "Just like his Uncle Vlad," Vlad says.

I nestle more tightly against his pants until he kicks me away.

Pat stops by the table, towing a big girl from Benson he's picked up. Her hair is in disarray. They had been making out by the aging Pac-Man table. Both of them look abstracted and inward, as though they've been through an accident.

"We're outta here," comments Pat. He raps on the table once, then with a guilty slouch, heads for the door.

"Well, well," Bob smirks, when they're barely out of range. "Another regret for the morrow."

"Yeah," agrees Vlad, punching an imaginary button on the table, "eject-a-bed."

The baby makes soft, sleepy noises. A train whistle builds in the distance, like an accordion being slowly crunched by a foot. The heat of Vlad's body washes through his pants and I push in closer. I imagine the three of us grouped together like a madonna and child and cherub, an odd family, but a cozy one. Up above, drinks arrive with the chiming of ice against glass. This is my favorite time of the evening, the swell before last call, a moment of warmth and vitality that feels like it could last forever, like it's packed with meaning. We are all encased in that golden bubble; even the coeds, even Gup Gup, propped at the bar, drinking a shimmering glass of eldritch scotch. We feel the promise that we will be whole, and alive, and satisfied.

Vlad sips his drink through a straw and watches the baby drowse in his arms.

"Check this guy out," he says, "he's breathing." He watches its body expand and contract with a kind of rapture. Then he bends and kisses it tenderly, on the knee.

The hand has made its way back to the plastic flowers. It crouches there like a flesh chrysanthemum, clutching its puttied fingers. I notice the other ghosts have started moving toward us, shambling from all corners of the bar, making their bitter, hulking way toward the baby and Vlad. It's like a zombie movie. The coeds crowd in first, leaning on their arms so their cleavage pops out. Then Gup Gup shuffles up, grinning through his yellowed eyeballs. In a second tier a ring of other assorted dead things push in, bandaged and bloody, like cheaply costumed movie extras. Of course *I'm* there, hopping under the table. Kicked and abused. We all nuzzle toward the unlikely pair, Vlad and the baby, curled together, the two of them sleepy and encrushed and content. Wanting to suck up some of that hope without crumbling our own sapless hearts. He brushes a petal of hair off a temple and lets his palm linger on the warm spot. The baby squirms under his touch. We can't believe how lucky he is.

There have been a few times, over the years, when a one-legged man of about the right age has hobbled in here. I think I would know him immediately. I imagine the feeling would flare up like love at first sight. When I look at those gimps and don't feel anything, I still think *maybe*. I mean, you don't wait, do nothing but wait, for nothing. So I check. I fit myself up against the gap: am I the correct height, given the passage of years? What's his shoe size? Do I feel anything when I touch him? Do I hear some sort of music?

I haven't heard anything yet.

We all push in closer toward Vlad and the baby, excited and envious. Like I said, ghosts want to be close to the living who remind us of ourselves. Not the selves we had, not exactly, but the ones we wished for. The repaired and shiny versions. The ones who didn't die on car seats, or in hallways with pay phones bolted to the walls, but who instead went on to get jobs and get married to swell gals, and to barbecue meat on Sunday afternoons in the backyard. The versions who got rescued, by ourselves or someone else. Who stopped drinking, or only drank a little now. Who went to bed and ate lunch and woke up feeling good, as good as we felt before last call.

It's always possible. Even in this soiled barroom tacked down to a windswept desert, on this pathetic street filled with auto repair shops, there might enter the miraculous mirage of the everyday—that like the baby we might be loved, and abandoned, and then suddenly loved again, all in the seamless roll of an evening.

Even Gup Gup feels it. Gup Gup especially, because he leans his jaundiced, swollen head in close, full of appetite. From the drained expression on Vlad's face I would bet something has gone wrong. Something must have shifted inside Vlad that's enabled him to, well—this is horrible—but he can *see* Gup Gup. Possibly smell him, I'd say, from the way he shrinks, curling his body protectively around the kid.

"Ghosts don't exist . . . Bob," he says evenly, "Bob? Are you getting this?"

"No," Bob says, "I haven't been getting it for a long time."

Vlad's eyes water with horror. I'm going out on a limb here, but I'd say he can see everything, our cellophane flesh, all of us cooing and wishful and predatory. The grasping hand, the perforated husband, and with a peek under the table, the sliced and bloody crown of me. Whom he kicks away.

"Holy shit," he says. Then: "Fuck."

He makes an odd bellow that doesn't involve opening his mouth, and looks at us with a sneer—a level of contempt Vlad usually reserves for people who drink Coors out of the can—so we all push closer, wanting to get the last of this, because it's obvious he's about to flee. He can't possibly come back. He has seen us, finally. He's seen the partial, broken versions of himself lurking in the future.

"Bob, are you with me?"

Bob is still immune. "I want to finish my drink. . . ."

In general, ghosts don't feel much. What's the point? But Vlad is the one. The only boy I adore. I watch him stand on those long legs and pilot himself toward the exit. Fleet of foot. He doesn't even think about it: trunk and limbs, it's all a single thing to him. He's carrying the baby in his arms carefully, like a box of wineglasses. He opens the door. The two of them make one silhouette against the light from the street.

He steps out into it.

Prom Night

IN THE BEGINNING was everything, and it was promised to us, but we didn't possess any of it yet. There was, for example, a gorgeous night perfumed with citrus blossoms, and we were in our gowns, driving drunk and on drugs. Somewhere there was a prom, and we wanted to go there. Our parents were so old that within their lifetimes they had put rubber bands around their kitchen doorknobs and watched them decay and fall off. I personally did not intend to live that long. I was prepared to perish glamorously after leading a brief, enchanted life punctuated by formal evenings, of which this would be the first of many.

I was lounging in the backseat beside my escort, Buck Panther. Nina was driving. She was the best of the four of us at driving on drugs. Whenever the cops stopped her, she would weep inconsolably until they let her go. Back then everyone was always letting us go. Nina wore a hot pink gown and a gardenia wrist corsage. I wore a black sixties cocktail dress and a gardenia wrist corsage. Somewhere in my deepest heart I believed I was Audrey Hepburn in *Breakfast at Tiffany's*. It was 1985, and I would be the only girl at the prom in black. Sometimes now I dream I'm at my ten-year reunion. All the other girls are wearing black, scattered across the floor like crows. Buck looks older, wasted and frail in his powder blue tux with a yellow IV tube snaking out of his arm.

Yet in the beginning nothing like that had happened to anyone we knew, and we were on cocaine, and we were floating toward the prom. Nina's date Mike was a year older than us and in the army. "Take this," he crooned, and handed me the loveliest blue pill, fuzzed with pocket lint. It was on my tongue and then gone.

I looked over at Buck. He and I had been dating for three months and hadn't done much more than kissed inside cars. We weren't anything yet, but when we were, he was going to be like Bono. He had a motorcycle, and was in a New Wave band, and on that night he looked especially handsome in his rented tuxedo, with his black hair slicked back on the sides and a slap of his dad's aftershave on either cheek. Around his head was a corona of bells, tinkling softly.

"Your bells are fabulous," I told him. "I love those fabulous, darling bells."

"My bells?" he asked.

We'd reached the parking lot of a large hotel. Nina and Mike had wandered ahead. Suddenly my back was against a station wagon and Buck was kissing me with kisses that made everything else smear together. My hands were inside his tuxedo jacket wrapped all the way around to the small of his back. The color of all this was deep, swimming pool blue. His body was warmer than any I'd ever touched, and for a minute I had a feeling, like he was a person.

"I have to . . ." he said, then leaned over and yawned a long, yellow rope of vomit onto the blacktop.

"Goodness," I said. "How dramatic! Do you think you're okay?"

"It must have been the pills I got out of my mother's medicine cabinet. I thought they were vitamins."

He had hit the petals of my wrist corsage so I flung it on the ground.

We walked through an archway, past a security guard peeling disks of baloney off a tray. In the vestibule we found a row of name tags pinned to the table like insects. Buck produced a pair of tickets and we stepped into a convention hall garnished with giant Indonesian shadow puppets.

"Bucky?"

"What?"

"Do you think we're going to remember this, Bucky?"

"We can get our picture taken," he said. "Then it won't matter."

Nina and Mike were dancing on a parquet floor. A quartet of men in matching vests toiled over musical instruments on the stage. The singer approached the microphone and spoke the words: "Wake me up before you go go." Bucky took my hand and led me onto the floor. I watched him while he stepped from side to side, haltingly, doing a rigor mortis–style undead dance.

"You dance divinely," I lied. All around us, smiling kids in formal wear bounced and whirled. I had never seen any of them before. "Don't we go to school here?" I asked, when the band lulled. "Aren't these supposed to be our classmates?"

"It's a big school," Buck said, with conviction. "It would be impossible for us to know everyone."

"But darling, shouldn't we know somebody?"

He pointed to the corner, where Nina and Mike stood absolutely still, like cardboard cutouts.

The singer stepped up to the microphone and peered over a sea of taffeta and hair. "You are so beautiful to me," he said.

Buck had begun his creaky, side-to-side routine again. I stood and watched. His name tag said "Constance." I looked down at my chest, where I sported the tag "Garth." A corsage had reappeared on my wrist.

Mike spun by. Nina was giggling and making the universal, two-finger hand signal for cigarette. I watched them whirl toward the lobby.

"Are we having fun yet?" said Buck. There was something not okay about his teeth. There was something not okay about his hands as well—they were covered with a pattern of half crescents, and gleaming.

"Do we feel all right?" I said.

"We might need to sit down."

This wasn't quite right either, because I was always the one telling Buck what needed to be done. We located some chairs. Complete strangers chatted over white tablecloths at the next table. All the girls wore pink. All the boys wore gray. It was quite stunning, really.

"Do you want me to remove your arm?"

"What?"

"Well, the bathroom is over there."

I began the long, long voyage across the ballroom,

walking step-together, step-together, like a bride. And I felt like a bride about to be wed to some terrible, overwhelming force, like a virgin preparing to be thrown into the volcano. There was something so wonderfully tragic about it all. My cocktail dress had two little trains cascading down the back. I felt them sweep behind me like vestigial wings.

In the stall I struggled with my gorgeous black stockings. They were the old-fashioned kind, with garters, very difficult. But they made me feel pretty.

Buck was outside the door waiting for me. "Sweetie," he said, and held out his arms. He looked strange, altered somehow, like what was inside his jacket wasn't actually his body. Those shoulders weren't really shoulders at all—perhaps molded Styrofoam replicas. I wondered exactly what kind of pills his mother kept in her medicine cabinet.

"You," I said. "You adorable scamp." We grasped hands. Beside us was a large statue of Buddha, two stories high, decorated with multicolored balloons.

Buck led me down a long hallway stuffed with red carpeting. Then we turned a corner and walked down another hallway. The carpet was so thick that our heels made a sucking sound when they came up. For the first time that evening, I began to feel a bit disoriented.

"I could just take something from you," he said as we walked, "if you wanted. Or I could kill you, if you wanted that."

"What?"

"What *what?*"

"No, what did you say?"

"Whatever you want." He pushed open the door to a

room. There was a red carpet and a white coverlet, and on the wall, a painting of lords and ladies dancing. Buck turned to me and smiled, a warm, all-American smile. The sides of his hair had begun to break free of the gel, and he looked like a curly-headed movie star. He looked wonderful, and scrumptious, and he was not himself. He was not Buck. Nor any person. This certainly was a bad thing.

"And what are we doing here, again?"

"Whatever you want," said the creature who resembled Buck. His hands were in my hair and he was kissing me. We were kissing each other, and I knew it wasn't Buck but I didn't care. I didn't want it to stop. The room had darkened, though it was bright in the corners. His body felt spongy. I was staring at his eyes, which looked like shiny new pennies, tails up. When I examined them more closely, I could make out the shadowy outline of the Lincoln Memorial, and inside, deeper, the little liquid figure of Abraham Lincoln tucked behind the columns.

He unzipped my dress and it slipped off my shoulders. The carpet swallowed it. His hands were very hot on my skin. "I'm not supposed to," I said. "I'm not supposed to want . . ." He pushed a tongue, or a tongue-like substance, into my mouth before I could finish saying, "I'm not supposed to want to fuck the Abraham Lincoln Monster."

But I did want to.

We were lying on top of the bedspread. Beneath his powder blue tuxedo pants the Abraham Lincoln Monster had a thick penis, plum black and decaying. I wanted to be affiliated with it even as it repulsed me. Then he was taking off my panties and pushing it inside me, and it hurt a lot but in an abstract way, and I was looking at his hands where they bore his weight, covered with those curious half-moons resembling copper fish scales.

"I didn't think it would go like this," I said, when he crawled off of me. I meant my virginity of course.

"Sweet sixteen," he replied, in a voice that wasn't even trying to be human anymore.

I assumed he meant our sweet sixteenth president.

"It's getting late," I was informed. The blue suit was back on, as though it had never been off. "I'll meet you in the car."

I stayed in the room for an hour or so, watching TV. There was a made-for-TV movie about a pretty young woman who was attacked by a razor-toothed doll. She seemed unable to figure out how to call for help or get away. For this stupidity she was eventually devoured.

I found Nina and Mike posing by the car smoking cigarettes with studied flair. Buck was passed out in back, breathing through his mouth.

"Is it over?" he asked, when I slid in beside him. "Did I miss the whole thing?" He was pitiful, of course, and quite himself.

"You got sick," I told him. "You took some pills from your poor mother and they made you ill."

"Are you mad at me?"

"Of course not," I said. "I had a wonderful time."

Nina started the car and we rolled into the warm, tar-scented night. Next to me, Buck's head lolled against the back of the seat. The color of all this was brown, a buff-mushroom brown.

Nina dropped me off in my driveway and I let myself

in with my key. In the kitchen, I found my little niece Sophie staggering around on the tile, wearing her footed pajamas. Her face was still creased from the blankets.

"I want my bunny," she announced.

"Goodness, sweetheart." We teetered into her room where I started to dig through a sack of stuffed animals. "How about this handsome fellow?" I pulled out a pony.

"No!" She was crying now. "He's a beautiful, beautiful bunny."

I kept rummaging but I couldn't find any bunnies, beautiful or otherwise.

"In the car," Sophie elaborated, her nose dripping onto her lip. "With ears . . . His ears were long." She gestured, making the universal hand signal for long bunny ears.

Then I remembered an inflatable rabbit we'd been given free with fill-up at a gas station when she had visited the year before. It was squat, with sharp, plastic edges that scratched crimson welts into her cheeks. Sophie dragged it with her everywhere and it had quickly turned brown. My sister had thrown it out.

"I don't think we have it anymore, cupcake."

"I want my beautiful, beautiful bunny," she sobbed, her entire head turning red, even her scalp. She cast her eyes around the room listlessly, intoxicated with grief. It was clear from this performance that nothing would ever be properly focused again.

So I got in my car and started driving over streets that had turned ratty and gray in the dawn. My gardenia wrist corsage was wilting and smelled faintly vomity. I tossed it out the window, thinking there would be other formal occasions. Yet that was my first and last. I checked every gas station and then every toy store, but I couldn't find a single beautiful blow-up bunny with sharp ears. Every-body kept telling me they didn't make them anymore. Or that they had never made them in the first place. Since then nothing has been promised to me. Since then every-thing has been my fault.

My Date with Satan

MY DATE with Satan commenced at the Sanrio store near Union Square where we went to browse through two stories of miniature Japanese school supplies and grooming accessories. Satan seemed nervous. "All the light," he said, "I don't like all the light." It's true the Sanrio store has a wide glass facade, glass doors, and a Plexiglas staircase to better illuminate the many rows of miniature Hello Kitty and Ahiru No Pekkle trinkets—endless, perfectly arranged rows of tiny colored pencils, mite-sized plastic address books, barrettes as small as aspirin—a thousand diminutive products to lodge in a thousand dinky airways. What do you think of that, Satan? What do you think of little kiddies choking on Sanrio brand Keroppi-Frog pencil erasers? Satan liked that very much and set to cackling and browsing and didn't seem so nervous once he had something evil to rest his mind on.

I voyaged deep into the Hello Kitty aisle and stared into

Kitty's pert Liza Minnelli eyes as they gazed back at me from a giant cat-shaped plastic display case, the only large object in the room. Inside its belly was tier upon tier of Hello Kitty dolls, arrayed like a scientific model of parasites invading a host. The display reminded me of a documentary I'd seen about a shrine in Japan stocked with ceramic cats with their paws raised—entreating, liquid-eyed cats. Supplicants would bring offerings of tuna and pray to Buddha for mercy on the souls of their lost pets. They'd burn incense in hope of drawing their cats home safely. This struck me as wildly funny and I went up to Satan, who was reading Sanrio product literature by the register, to tell him about the shrine in Japan for wayward cats.

Satan was laughing maniacally. "Look here," he said, thrusting a magazine at me. "There's this interview with the lady who invented all these Sanrio characters, and the guy asks her, 'To what do you attribute the success of your creation Hello Kitty?' and the lady replies, 'She has no mouth you see.'"

He threw back his head and laughed some more.

A crowd of children had started to gather around Satan and me, pointing at my hair, which I had done up in braids entwined with wire so they stuck out of my head at right angles like my namesake, Pippi Longstocking, or PipiLngstck as I am known onscreen. Also, I was wearing a pinafore over a white smock and Buster Brown shoes; these may have attracted the children as well. Satan appeared more kosher in terms of what is acceptable in San Francisco. He was wearing a black trench coat, a black silky shirt, Gap jeans, and black Reeboks—he looked dorky, to tell the truth, like a brooding loser outcast guy. His Paul McCartney bowl cut was the clincher. Still, there's nothing I love better than loser outcast guys, as I'd told Satan when I first met him in LE CHATEAU, brooding in the corner, trying to get someone to notice him.

"You're exactly the kind of guy I would have had a crush on in high school," I said. He threw bits of chalk at me for the next twenty minutes. Not actually throwing, as we were communicating in a computer chat room, LE CHATEAU, the SM meeting place, but rather, periodically typing in the phrase: *"Lobbing another piece of chalk at PipiLngstck's head."* And I'd type back, *"Ouch, Satan, that hurts. You're a very bad boy!"* Then Satan would throw a notebook at me. So I'd say, *"Satan, do you have to be taken outside and spanked?"* And Satan would type back, *"Oh, I love you, PipiLngstck."* I'd say, *"I don't want LOVE from such a nasty boy. I want OBEDIENCE!!!"*

Then he'd ignore me for a while while other people in LE CHATEAU, Domin8U, subBoy, or LaraLee tried to pick me up. *"Are you brooding, Satan?"* I'd ask. Satan would make weak excuses for his behavior, saying stuff like, *"Forgive me, dove, it's the solitude, the incessant solitude, that has made me this way."* Occasionally he'd lapse into stilted, romantic-medieval blather: *"PipiLngstck, I see you bearing down upon me in a flowing robe, thighs flashing, a dagger in your hand. You strike for my neck and leave me tattered, bleeding, devastated."*

"You're not one of those geeks who likes Renaissance fairs, are you, Stan?" (If you want to get Satan really mad, call him Stan.)

"A geek for love."

Then I shoved Satan into a private room, where no one else on the system could see what we typed, and told him exactly what I was doing to him, blow by blow.

• • •

I was hoping for something wholesome on my date with Satan; maybe not exactly wholesome, but I was wearing a stiff, white Playtex bra like somebody's second-grade teacher might wear and I wanted to bring Satan to the Sanrio store so we could look at all the miniature products in their ingenious packaging arranged so perfectly and orderly on the shelf, all the edges lining up. All of it was so cute and perky it stirred up some kind of answering violence in me, the violence of white cotton underwear, of Catholic schoolgirls, of PipiLngstck and cookies and milk. I told Satan how there's a saying in Japan—people might say this of an infant or a baby animal—*he's so cute I want to hit him on the head with a hammer.* Satan *really* liked that. He said he knew all about that. When he laughed he looked pretty damn cute himself. His hair was too long and falling into his eyes; there was some baby fat left around his chin even though he claimed to be twenty-five, same as me. He was jumping around the store totally hyper, pointing at Hello Kitty and going, "BAM," like he was braining her and chanting: "She has no mouth, you see."

"Chill, Satan, they'll kick us out."

"Fair lady, who cares?" Satan leered and I thought he was going to kiss me. I took a giant step backward. Even though I'd done everything I could think of to him in private rooms on the computer, I didn't think it proper for him to kiss me just yet. We still had a lot to learn about each other. He'd made *that* pitifully clear on the phone when he'd said that his idea of a perfect date was to drink a couple of beers while watching *The Lost Boys* with a lassie in latex pants slumped next to him on the couch.

My dream date, on the other hand, involved the perky sterility of the Sanrio store.

"She has no mouth, you see," Satan said, again. "No mouth, no expression. She could be feeling anything, that's what the lady said, though I'm not convinced Kitty is a lassie. There seems to be no indication down there"—he flipped the doll over—"so that little Timmy can imagine Kitty is smiling, crying, or smoking crack! Whatever so pleases him, to match his very own mood!" He leapt across the aisle and knocked a Spottie Dottie dental hygiene set onto the floor. "The secret of success. No mouth!"

I dragged Satan out of there with the sales staff (whose duty it was to be peppy in all circumstances) looking pissed off. We walked up Stockton toward the Chinatown tunnel. We had a plan to go to Satan's favorite dim sum shop. The whole date was very organized. While we waited to cross the street, Satan reached into his coat and pulled out a stuffed Hello Kitty doll. "For you, dove."

"For me? You stole this for me?"

I was wearing eyeliner. He was wearing eyeliner too.

At the dim sum take-out shop Satan ordered nothing but those long, slimy noodles in beef sauce that have the same heft and texture as a human tongue. I ordered a variety of items, including pork buns and shrimp balls. Satan snorted when I said "pork buns." By then, I noticed, I was starting to get sick of him.

We took our food outside and sat on the sidewalk with our shoes in the gutter. "For you, dove," Satan said, pulling a pair of chopsticks out of his pocket.

I watched him suck noodles into his mouth. "All one thing, isn't that a little, uh, extreme? For a meal intended as a series of appetizers?"

Satan shifted his food into his cheek. "I have an attraction to extremes, fair Pippi."

"Oh, yeah. I second that."

"If it's not extreme," he continued, "I mean, what's the point?" He stared into crates of cabbage and unripe mangos overflowing onto the sidewalk. "When you eat on the street in Chinatown," Satan observed, "people look at you like you're a dog eating out of the gutter."

It was true, I noticed, people did shoot us dirty looks, but I was used to it. All the bosses I'd ever had seemed to regard me as disposable tissue that typed: ordering me around, snickering behind my back, seeming more amazed when I did a job well than when I did one badly. Maybe it was my unusual personal appearance—the fact that I drew freckles on my cheeks with eyeliner or daubed teardrops under my eyes with mascara, or that my braids stuck out at right angles from my head; or maybe it was the short skirts, white bobby socks, and cardigan sweaters I often wore. Or my high, little-girl voice. I don't know. It seemed like there were plenty of people in San Francisco who dressed artistically, you'd think even people with power would get over it. But I was forced to suffer indignities. At one office, before I quit to become a temp, I was told to sign a ten-point CODE OF BEHAVIOR or else CLEAN OUT MY DESK. These points included: no toothbrushing in common areas, no cavorting in skirts short enough to reveal undergarments, no wearing of little stuffed birds in the hair.

All I wanted was to look sweet and wholesome. I

wanted to have some sort of access to the land of puppies and bunnies and things that are good and simple and true. I wanted the goodness to seep inside me so I would be good and simple and true myself. This way I could keep everything in order; I could be sad at certain times and happy at others. Some nights I dreamed I was throwing live kittens at moving cars, choking with rage. When I woke up I'd still feel out-of-sorts, so I might go into the bathroom before work and draw on a grin, or add big eyelashes and spot my cheeks with roses. That would mean I was happy. Or draw on tears—then I was sad again. It all had a linear cause and effect that calmed me and made me a better worker, in my opinion.

"Satan, are you cold?" The afternoon was mild, but Satan hunched on the curb with the collar of his trench coat turned up, sucking noodles into his mouth.

"The chill is within my soul, lady."

It was sort of disturbing to watch him eat. He wasn't very good with the chopsticks. "Now that you've met me, Satan, what do you think?"

He eyed me coolly. He wasn't as eager in real life as he was onscreen. In fact, he was kind of arrogant. "I think you're pretty."

"I told you I was pretty."

"Computers lie."

"Computers don't lie. People using computers lie."

"Guns don't kill people, people kill people."

"You're real snappy, Satan. A real snappy guy. Aren't you going to ask me if I like you?"

"No." He grinned that sassy grin. "I can tell you like me."

I squealed and grabbed him by the hair. He was right.

At that point, I knew about one thing for sure about Satan: he was a geek. He had the queer, stylized diction, the mannered exterior, the inability to make eye contact, that screamed of geekdom. Geek! He was, I decided, one of those guys who had been obsessed with role-playing games like Dungeons and Dragons in high school; misfits shamed into lives of fantasy by the scarlet bubbles of acne percolating across their faces. They had to take on the role of Sir Quidball or Fatemaster or The Lad Ambrose and pretend to seize the opal from the high tower or something if they were ever going to be able to converse with another human being. But now all those guys need is a computer and a modem and they can just log on and avoid showing their faces altogether.

I thought it was nice. Someone could type: "*I'm grinding my pelvis into your face and yanking up on your hair,*" into a keyboard, and everyone would get hard and wet and come or whatever in the privacy of their own homes. I really hate it when people, usually the older generation, say how technology is depersonalizing and makes us into machines and the future is dank and scary. I mean, first of all, I see plenty of people in real life, and secondly, it's not like people on the computer are fake. They're out there. I knew Satan as the sweet boy who licked my boots and called me Mistress of the Doves. When he found out we both lived in the Bay Area, he was beside himself with excitement.

"*Please,*" he typed, "*if I could feast my eyes on you but once fair lady, all my existence would be complete.*"

"*I don't know, Satan,*" I typed back, "*it could spoil everything.*"

"*Lady, I think about you day and night,*" he replied. "*It doesn't seem like there would be any point in getting up in the morning, or that my pathetic life would be worth living at all, if I missed the chance to touch you, even once."*

So there we were, on a date, dating. My date with Satan.

We went back to his place. "His place" isn't the term, exactly, because "due to unusual circumstances where my presence and my responsibility are often unexpectedly required," as he put it, Satan lived at home with his mother and sister.

"Mom's out today," he said, as we climbed the stairs. "And sister's always out."

It was a deluxe apartment on the top story of a Victorian in North Beach, a very fancy address. He led me into a big open room with a view of the bay and the Golden Gate, all that tourist stuff. They had a piano with a bowl of real fruit on it. Satan hunched over it and started to play "Some Enchanted Evening."

"Nice pad, Satan." I had an urge to defile the place.

"Yes, my sweet, I call it home. Come, allow me to escort you on the grand tour."

Satan began to lead me around the apartment. He showed me the kitchen, the balcony, the den, and then his room. I knew Satan was a respectable guy with a job as a programmer at some hot shit firm in Berkeley but, well, I guess I wasn't surprised to see he lived with his mom with only one place as a refuge—his room. It was all decked out with Star Trek posters, shelves of William Gibson and Anne Rice books, a slick computer with every available peripheral. We made a loop and ended up back in the front room. Satan stopped on a little step below me and looked at me with hungry, velvet eyes. I grabbed his chin and kissed him hard on the mouth. He sank to his knees and began lapping at my ankles.

I have no idea why I elicit this from men. Every boy I've ever known has wanted to put on an apron and high heels in my honor and scrub my sink with Comet, or wear a collar with a leash threaded through his nipple rings and have me pull him around the floor. They want to be turned over my knees with their pants pulled down and be spanked, paddled, and whipped. They want to lick my boots and roll over on their backs and pee on themselves like cowed beta wolves. There seems to be something about me. I have a markedly little-girl style I admit. I've been told I look like a little lost orphan by bus drivers, store clerks, and ticket vendors. There must be some kind of magnetic attraction in this, to be flailed at by a full-grown girl in a pink romper. Maybe they think I can't really hurt them.

I'll confess I don't really mind. I mean, I kind of enjoy it, and it seems to mean so much to them. It's like they open their souls, they get so sweet and vulnerable. I don't have to do anything really. Half the time they don't ask for anything from me. I just stand there and say, "You slut, you love it," or whatever seems right, and they tell me all their secrets. They weep and say they love me.

In this case Satan and I had already practiced on the screen so I knew exactly what kind of scenes were flitting through his mind. I was composing a list in my head of things I was going to do to him, there on the stairs with Satan groveling at my feet, when a little girl about six years old pounced into the room chased by a woman.

"Shit," said Satan, standing up. "What'd you have to bring her in here for?"

"You try and stop her," said the woman. She dropped to her knees and started to crawl toward the little girl.

The girl jumped into the center of the room. One blue eye looked at me while the other wandered up the wall. She was pretty I thought, with wild, blue-black hair and little hands balled up in fists. She had on a sequined body suit with a stiff ruffle pouching out around her waist, like a ballet costume.

"She's so cute," I said. "A little fairy thing. What is she, your sister?"

"Yeah," Satan said quietly.

"Well, she's cute."

"She can't help it," Satan said. "Let's go into my room."

The little girl stared ahead with glassy eyes. "Are you a real little girl?" I asked.

"Are you a real little girl?" she said back.

"Or are you a fairy?"

"Or are you a fairy?"

"I'm the Queen of the fairies," I told her, bending closer, "and I want to know if you're one of us."

"If you're one of us." She looked at me with vacant panic.

"I get it, it's a game. What's your name, honey?"

The little girl stared at me, but it felt like she was looking through my head.

"Her name is Ivy," the woman said. She had a fancy haircut and a young face but she seemed so annoyed and responsible that I thought she must be an employee.

"She's a doll. I want one."

"Can we get her out of here?" Satan was nervous. He began to edge toward the little girl from the side while the woman—the maid I guess—snuck up from behind. As soon as he was within reach the girl began to scream.

"Fuck!" yelled Satan.

"My God, what did you do to her?"

"I didn't do anything to her," he said, in a weary voice, "she's just like this. There isn't really anything to do to her."

The girl sat on the floor and started doing something that looked like she was shooing invisible flies off her nose, over and over.

"Come on, Pippi. Nancy's supposed to be taking care of her anyway."

When we started to leave the room the little girl began to scream again; piercing, vicious, cat snarls.

"Please," the lady said, "please?" She gave Satan a long, pathetic, entreating look. "If I have to deal with this all day, they'll have to put *me* in an institution."

"No way," Satan said. "I have a guest."

Long, rhythmic shrieks issued from the little girl. The lady sank to the floor.

Satan dragged himself to the piano. "You owe me, Nancy. You owe me big." He made some curlicues up in the high notes. "And now, ladies and gentlemen," he addressed the back of the piano, a classy baby grand, "a serenade to the diminutive tyrant of the household." Satan's head drooped and his hair fell over his face. He played a slow, mournful introduction, buried under Ivy's wails, then began to sing: "*Mommy's blue*"—oh! a Billie Holiday song!—"*. . . because her little girl is going on* *three. . . .*" He had a low, trembling voice, "*but Miss Amanda she's as proud as can be. . . .*"

Satan was swaying, his eyelids drooping, looking so natural and self-conscious at once I felt like running out of the room. It all seemed so, I don't know—complicated. Instead I looked at the little girl, the delightful little Ivy-girl, shrieking now in raspy hiccups. The music seemed to relax her. Her hands uncurled and she focused on my knees, staggering toward them, arms extended in front of her like a baby version of Frankenstein, aiming directly for the Hello Kitty hanging out of my hand.

"She wants my doll."

"Oh God," Satan said, but he kept playing.

"Just let her have it," the woman implored.

"No!" Satan jumped up. "She'll fuck with it!"

The little girl began screaming anew. What vocal cords! The glass in the window frames rattled. Satan resumed playing and she quieted. Ivy began pulling on Hello Kitty's leg.

"Just give it to her," he told me, "the little fascist. Otherwise we'll be here forever. You can't believe her endurance. Sorry. I'm really sorry."

Satan played on. I handed the girl the doll and she set upon it, tearing its belly along the sharp edge of the coffee table, ripping a big gash in Kitty's stomach with a methodical violence, a strange mixture of purpose and detachment.

"*You're a big girl now. . . .*" Satan sang, as Ivy, with muffled gasps, pulled spun stuffing out of Kitty's body cavity and tossed it onto the floor.

"God, why is she doing that?"

"Ivy has a thing about dolls," Satan said, his fingers

moving across the keys. "She has to get inside of them. She thinks there's something in there."

"We think she's looking for their feelings. People with her disorder have trouble with emotions."

"What's wrong with her?"

"She's autistic," said the woman.

"Oh. Will she always be like that?"

"I don't know," she said. "No one really knows."

Ivy had calmed down—she was flinging bits of fiber into the air and watching them descend through the light, enraptured. The woman was able to pick her up and carry her from the room. My Kitty lay deflated, her polyester feelings strung out across the hardwood floor.

"I regret the interruption," Satan said. "Accept my apologies. And now, my dear, allow me to escort you into the inner sanctuary."

Satan was striped with gaffer's tape and he wanted me to rip it off. When I kissed him and ran my hands under his shirt I discovered the plastic slickness of the tape encasing him like armor. I removed his clothes to discover he was crosshatched on his chest and buttocks and thighs.

"Jesus, Satan, that's going to make you yelp."

"Fair princess, to feel pain at your hands is but the greatest pleasure." He was spread out on top of his bed, trembling, surrounded by computers and high school banners and a big poster of a blond lady riding a horse through a Day-Glo medieval forest.

"Well, you might flinch. We'll have to prevent that," I said, and began to tie Satan to the posts of his bed with laundry I picked off the carpet. My braids kept getting in the way so I twisted them together behind my neck. "You look so cute, I want to hit you on the head with a hammer."

"Don't make me wait," said Satan, a catch in his voice, so I hopped astride him and tore one leg of a chest-sized X off his skin, a clean rip from nipple to belly.

He screamed.

I turned over the tape and examined the hairs embedded in it. It had left a tender pink swath across Satan's chest. Dots of blood welled from his pores.

"That looks pretty rough, kiddo. Are you up for this? Maybe we should start a little slower."

"Don't turn pussy on me now," he said. I told him he was asking for it and pulled off the other half of the X.

Satan screamed. He had quite a hard-on. "We'll see who's a pussy now," I said, working methodically, tearing the smaller sections of tape off his thighs and legs rhythmically. He eventually stopped screaming and simply lay there trembling.

"I'm completely at your mercy. I'm yours. Do with me as you will. Rip me open. I am like one of Ivy's dolls if you so desire, my lady."

I wrapped my hand around his thing.

He said, "I love you."

"Yeah, I know."

"No really, I love you really. God, I can't believe this is happening. I feel like we've known each other forever."

I slid his penis into my mouth and he actually kept talking:

"It's just a computer, I know, but it's so real. I can tell so much about you by what you write. You don't know how many times I've pictured you here with me. Ferris. My real name is Ferris. What's your real name?"

I relaxed my lips and let my teeth scrape against him. Whenever a guy gets all earnest and yearning like that, my enthusiasm for sex just clots. Sometimes I think they go out of their way to disgust me. I gave his penis one last gnaw and spat it out.

"I don't have a real name." I took a flap of silver tape without much stick left to it and put it over my mouth. "I have no mouth, you see."

"Hey, please, come on. I love you. I'd be on my knees if I weren't tied up. I'd kiss your feet. I mean," his eyes filmed over, "I really love you. So tell me your real name? I'm begging?"

My eyes trailed across the pink and trembling figure of Satan, bound. Ferris, now he'd want me to call him *Ferris.* I don't know why this always has to happen to me. Guys always reach the point where they want me to take out my braids, wipe off my makeup, dress like other girls, "real girls," they say. They want me to tell them my name, my address, my social security number; they want to open me up like a package and crawl around inside and find out exactly what's wrong with me and fix it and love it and I don't know why the hell they don't lay off. I don't know where they get off thinking I'm going to give up all my secrets, hand my life up over to some guy, a stupid guy who doesn't even have his own apartment. Who lives with his mother.

"You know what, Ferris?" I said cheerfully. "Fuck you."

His face fell. "Oh God, what did I do?"

Because there isn't any problem until they think there's a problem. There isn't any problem until they want to know what's inside me and then the problem is *they are all fucked up.* If they want a piece of me, I figure they must be empty to start with, right? Once they get started, where will it end? Before you know it I'll be married and living in the suburbs, fretting over carpet stains. I'll be one of those hollowed-out zombie wives, filling up a grocery cart, dimly wondering how I ever let some guy lure me into his little dream life. I've found the only thing to do in these cases is to leave. PipiLngstck is an expert in the delicate art of cutting her losses.

I left him on the bed, tied up and gunked with white adhesive residue. He had a decent chance, I decided, of working himself free before anyone (i.e., his mom) found him.

"Pippi," he whimpered, "you're leaving? Will I see you again on-line?"

Some guys, I've found, are like that: the colder PipiLngstck is to them, the more they think they have to have her.

On my way out, I decided to try to find the baby girl. I just wanted to say good-bye. I couldn't get over how adorable she looked in her princess dress, tearing up my Kitty doll in a trance. I poked around until I found her, alone in a room, staring at the pink and blue wallpaper like it was television. The water was running in the bathroom. She was so precious. Why was I always the one to leave empty-handed? I wrapped my arm around her little waist and dragged her with me down the stairs.

A Groupie, a Rock Star

A GROUPIE, a rock star. A pair of wicker loungers beside a pool. In the pool, a dead boy floats, face-down, his long hair fanning around his head like pond algae. True to form, he has died from injecting a large portion of distilled juice from a beautiful poppy into his foot. At almost any other time Connie, the groupie, would be doing everything in her power to make herself agreeable to Eldon, the rock star, a guitar player vaguely monstrous to look at. Only by virtue of being famous could a guy like Eldon get a girl as beautiful as Connie to spit on him, much less behave in an ingratiatingly cute and deferential manner toward him at all times. At this particular moment, however, Connie's cuteness has been preempted by rage. Her teeth are gritted and all the blood in her body is pumping into her head.

"Fuck," she yells, hitting Eldon with a soft little fist. "What the fuck is wrong with you?"

Connie has red hair and red lips and everything about

the way she looks is perfect. Eldon has become used to her pairing his socks and spooning the right amount of sugar into his coffee and can't understand how anything he might do or fail to do could possibly displease her. He started the band when he was twenty, and most matters related to personal responsibility have for years been siphoned from his jurisdiction by a clique of handlers and a group of sleazy boys Eldon refers to as his *entourage.* The most challenging part of his initiation into manhood involved learning to enjoy the taste of liquor.

"What?" he says, indignant, hunching to avoid her blows. "I didn't do it."

And it's true, he didn't. The boy's name is John, or it was John, and he was the kind of person who liked to carry things for other people, at least for other people who were famous. He was shy, and around the band he strained to make hip, trenchant comments—"Man, that solo blows my hair back"—or else not speak at all. He was one of an endless series of hangers-on who sort of worked for the band, or were close to people who worked for the band, and when the facts were finally discussed later, no one really knew if he had any official capacity or not. Also, no one seemed to know if he'd dedicated himself to drug use or if he was just experimenting.

To Eldon, these facts are yet unknown. He has already sent home the group of people he pays to manage emergencies and interpret the world for him—the manager, his lawyer, the buddies with official titles (wine taster, billiards expert, valet). His entourage has been dismissed because he's bought a set of leather restraints and a little whip, and he's hoping to use them for sexual purposes with Connie. It's unclear whether or not Connie is "into" this, or indeed if she even knows about it. She is as a rule so pliable and grateful for his attention that such matters don't find the need to be discussed ahead of time.

The two of them are unaccompanied, as they rarely are, relaxing beside Eldon's swimming pool, which is surrounded by a deck of glass brick and gold tile, which is surrounded by a lawn, which is sheltered by a ranch house on a large lot in the Hollywood Hills, California. In their glasses, ice cubes melt. There's a dead fellow in the pool, but actually they don't discover him right away. First they make out for a while and Connie sort of falls asleep, from a Valium she's taken earlier, making her subsequent burst of rage all the more astonishing.

Eldon, who has buried his chin in Connie's neck and inserted his hand beneath her shirt, where it makes a few lazy, half-assed attempts at undoing her bra, suspects Connie might be nodding off but he isn't sure. He finds her kind of freaky, like she's of a completely different species than he is, and attributes this to her excruciatingly good looks. Perhaps he even considers the restraints a contraption for containing the strangeness that is Connie. He's a little afraid of her, actually, and when he's most intimidated by her icy loveliness he says to himself: *Any chick who goes out with some dude just because he's in a band has got to be pretty dumb.*

Still, he hasn't had the nerve to pull the restraints out just yet, though in his mind he's already tied Connie to a structure made of rebar, then flayed her with the small whip—the whipette. He's not sure he'd really enjoy this kind of exercise in itself but he's pretty positive he'd enjoy the part where Connie starts to cry and he must ask for forgiveness. Then she takes him in her arms and forgives him. The tang of remorse is weird but addictive, like green olives, which he detects on Connie's lips as he sucks at her limp mouth and wonders if she might not be totally comatose. He reaches behind her to flip on the pool light, hoping to get a view of her, but instead illuminates John, bobbing softly in the water.

Eldon continues working on Connie's bra, even though he can see her eyes are half closed—not in a sexy way but an unconscious one—because something about the juxtaposition of elements is really working for him and he just feels turned on. Her stomach is soft and warm. She's like a sack of heated gravel in his arms. Ten feet away, a dead thing floats; while up above, demoralized by the wattage of greater LA, a half-moon garnishes the sky.

While he flails at the hooks he's hit by a premonition that other people might interpret this particular sexual thrill as bad or wrong, though for the moment, he doesn't give a shit. He's kicked free from morality. Eldon has a tendency to believe he's either a worm-like creature who deserves to be stepped on and humiliated and scrubbed very firmly with strong soap, or else to believe he's a famous rock star and a demigod and a magnet for envy. Something about having a dead boy in the pool makes him feel famous, and to have fame means morality no longer applies to him. It's the mental equivalent of diplomatic plates. It's this freedom, in the main, that gives the tableau its smutty tone. Because if he isn't responsible, he can do anything. He's freed from the normal range of sexual insecurities as a generation of rock stars had been freed before him. Like that rumor Led Zeppelin fucked a girl with a frozen halibut, and she fucking loved it. Or maybe she didn't love it, but the point is that Led Zeppelin could fuck anyone with anything because Jimmy Page was a legendary guitar player and he, Eldon, is also a legendary guitar player, though in a lesser way. He can therefore fuck Connie with a halibut or a whipette or a hairbrush and she would fucking love it, perhaps, or at least keep quiet if she didn't.

Connie slithers from Eldon's lap, where he's been making an effort to balance her. Her feet thump off the wicker chaise and onto the deck, a tile-and-glass-block affair with brightly colored plastic fish embedded in the glass. For a second Eldon doesn't really register what's happening with Connie because he's gone back to looking at John, floating in the pool, his hair fanning around his head like drowned weeds, and he's moved on to having a slight twinge—a spasm of regret—that Jimmy Page probably also had while fucking that groupie with a halibut. He's considering the idea that maybe a license to fuck anyone with anything is a diminishment of sorts, because you only had to be a legend to do it, and to be a legend automatically crowded out the possibility of being yourself. This he finds alarming. He's ready to handle remorse—remorse is a blue drip hitting his forehead; he's at the center, always—but regret seems to demand action or thought or a vantage point that might include someone else. So he begins to picture how he looks: himself, famous, sitting with a stoned groupie half off his lap by a big swimming pool shaped like a giant electric guitar and cleaned by Mexican gardeners who can't speak English but know all the words to his hit songs. On the bottom of the pool, in red tile, beneath John's pelvis, the word "Fender."

Without much provocation, the rest of Connie's body

oozes off the chaise longue until her face comes to rest gently against the deck. If she were to open her eyes she'd see brightly colored fish wedged inside glass blocks, and also a few toy soldiers and some dolls' heads that had been thrown in along with some miniature plastic furniture so that each block contained a demented little world where pink cod and uniformed men could kick back, relax, and converse with a body part; but as it turns out, when she finally opens her eyes she looks to the side, at the water, and sees John afloat.

Connie believes she's looking at a pair of pants somebody shucked into the water. Then she blinks and focuses and begins to understand that these pants are attached to a torso and a head. The thing, she notes with horror, is a figure, floating hands up, as if he's urging someone on the bottom of the pool to toss him a ball. Connie, in general, shares Eldon's view on the unlimited personal license of rock stars. This relieves her of the burden of making distinctions about his behavior, for which she's grateful; anyway, she's calibrated her existence on the belief that her boyfriend Eldon is at once very cool and basically absent as a fellow human being. But after she identifies John as a body, and notices Eldon watching the boy with the same bored, bemused lift of an eyebrow he reserves for country music and fat girls in tight clothes, she concludes that he's probably been aware of the corpse for a while. The boy looks so expectant, and it's so painfully true that the ball he's waiting for will never be tossed, that Connie is forced to abandon her rule of not making distinctions about Eldon and quickly adopts this one: his behavior in this matter is obviously blameworthy and probably sociopathic. He has killed the boy or done something equally evil in the act of looking at him without feeling. It's true that she herself often looks at Eldon without feeling, but this is something she handles with Valium or Xanax or Demerol or martinis and besides, she's never wanted to be girlfriend to a sociopath, and who knows what anyone really is, inside? He could be a serial killer. She didn't know about anyone. She might be a serial killer too.

"Fuck," she yells. She's already on her feet. And she hits him.

The odd result this produces is that for a moment, Eldon stops seeing Connie as an inscrutable ice queen. The blow doesn't hurt; instead, it snaps him to the understanding that Connie has a body, she's made of it—not in a sexy way (though her bra's off now and the goods, which are perfect, show through her half-unbuttoned blouse), but in the same way that as a child he'd only fully grasped the fact that his sister had a body when he doused her leg with lighter fluid and touched her with a match. He'd been angling for something like the footage he'd seen on TV of Vietnamese monks lit up like Bics, but the shrieks of his sister and the smell of her burning skin were so vivid that he, too, was taken ill and couldn't get out of bed for two days. The proximity of John's corpse heightens this—that he and Connie are alive is proved by the absolute suspension of the boy, his face brightened from below by the submerged light. He's like one of those figurines at that rip-off wax museum on Hollywood Boulevard that housed a dusty group of celebrities made of some plastic substance that sure as hell wasn't wax. Or it's like discovering that Connie isn't made of wax but some other polymer.

Connie is having similar waves of physical feeling

brought on by the floating body of John, who in life had been friendly, with chubby cheeks, and the inside of his mouth was pink. She touched him once, backstage, when she asked him to get her a pack of cigarettes. She remembers pressing him on the arm, in a springy spot above his elbow. He'd said something like, "I'll get you a pack of those bad boys." Then they looked at each other. In retrospect that look seemed hotter and more real than any full-blown sexual encounter she'd ever had with Eldon. In fact, Eldon appears ghostly in the rippling light coming off the pool, like a guy in the back row of Chemistry Club in a washed-out yearbook photo. It's kind of great, really. She'd always wanted a rock star; the particulars of the man hadn't mattered. She had just longed to be part of something vast, golden, and vaguely male. She had an empty slot in her life, or her heart, or pussy, or something, and it seemed like some really cool rocker could fill it up. Talent and fame were rare fluids that could never spring from inside her. But she could extract them, like semen, from her boyfriends.

But as it turned out, being a groupie meant living in someone else's eclipse. It meant picking his shirts out of pools of bourbon and rinsing his mythical fluids out of her hair; and so the draining implication of Eldon's responsibility for John's death—that he might in fact be a very bad man—is an exhilarating one. For the first time in months, Connie feels detached from him, like a barnacle that's been dislodged from the back of a whale. She is falling toward the ocean floor.

They've ended up beside one another, on their feet, staring at the body. This is when Connie allows herself to entertain the obvious fact that Eldon might in no way be responsible for the death of the boy, who may, like some other guys she'd known, have simply made an incredibly bad decision. He'd decided to inject so much juice from the beautiful poppy into his foot that he could no longer distinguish between sleeping in a deck chair, with the air all around him, and sleeping on the bottom of the pool, surrounded by water. This fact, to Connie, is such a sad one, such a cold, chemical-blue thought, that she can't have it more than once. To see that sadness, and to be beside Eldon, is intolerable. She prefers to blame Eldon, and stand away from him.

She walks to the other side of the pool, her bare feet making a soft whup, whup, whup on the tile. She side-steps around the neck of the guitar and stops beside a rack of croquet mallets. The mallets aren't for croquet, exactly, but for a made-up game involving drinking that Eldon and his buddies like to play in the maze winding from the west end of the deck to the high wall bordering the property. The maze is comprised of panels about five feet high that have been painted red and gold by the same artist who'd designed the entire patio area with one eye on the baroque and another one on some lame, watered-down version of pop art favored by Eldon. At one end the maze is embellished by a giant, cast-bronze ear, as tall as Connie, with a pleated outer cup leading to a hinged middle ear (complete with moving parts) tapering to a coiled cochlea crammed full of wooden croquet balls no one had been able to dislodge, though a drifter named Wolf once tried to burn them out.

Eldon can look at the ear, but he can no longer picture himself in relation to Connie. He can look at her, he can look at the boy in the pool, but he can no longer assemble this into a picture that shows things the way he'd like to have them shown, in a way where Eldon is always in the spotlight. Connie is no longer *his* groupie, as John is no longer his roadie or toady or lackey or whatever the hell it was he'd been. The problem seems to be that the three of them have mapped out a triangle of uncomfortable intensity that doesn't involve matters of stardom or fawning or power chords or publicity shots, but has to do instead with basic notions of life and death. He's a little nostalgic for the moment when Connie was on his lap and he could check out John without feeling much of anything, except famous. But some combination of the slap Connie gave him, and the night air, and the moonlight struggling through the smog has altered that. His stomach floods with the comprehension that John was animate but has now stopped. His own talent is not so much that he's famous or a wicked guitar player or a magnet for the vixens but that for forty-one years he has continually been in the habit of exhibiting life.

He's exhibiting life and Connie, with her tits hanging out of her shirt, is doing the same. That they share this property seems wild and a little nauseating. It ceases being significant that she looks perfect in every way. What's important is that little buzz, that piece of her that's good to go. It's amazing, but deflating too, like maybe her beauty has lost its market value.

Then he sort of thinks he doesn't really like her very much anymore.

Eldon hasn't yet considered the possibility that these alternating currents are a form of panic, a response to the fact that they're going through something together—a tragedy, which presents an opportunity for closeness that stinks of doom and their parents and boredom and the suburbs and divorce.

And when he does consider it, he retreats more deeply into his thoughts, hoping they can simply get through the tragedy at the same time, rather than together.

Eldon thinks about how much he doesn't need Connie. For the past six months, since they'd been hanging out regularly, Eldon has been telling people that Connie is a special lady, that she's his main muse, and that their liaison has inspired his hit song "Forever Needing You." But in truth Eldon had written that song one night after talking to his parents. When his dad got on the line he kept asking when was he going to get a "real job," as though gold records and chicks and acoustic sets on MTV comprised some sort of dim half-existence sapped of validity. In a way Eldon believed this, actually; he sort of believed everything his parents told him about himself, even as he disagreed violently, and this discrepancy produced a confused suffering that spurred him to write his most poignant songs, which in turn made the band more successful, which for some mysterious reason infuriated his father and pushed the two of them deeper into the realm where everything recedes like the last chorus fading out on the last song on a double album, a flop forever consigned to the cut-out bins.

His father would be so satisfied, Eldon thinks, when the press gets ahold of this. If he was damaged badly enough by the publicity, maybe his dad would go a few rounds of golf with him.

Connie crouches on the opposite side of the pool, gazing down at John and trying to find a graceful way to avoid the increasingly obvious fact that they're incredibly alike. She too is a hanger-on. She too is disposable. She contains a dead part that relies on some artificial light source to be seen. And Eldon didn't seem like such a luminous goddamn lantern anymore anyway. He was perishable. He could die, or find some other girl to do, and then she'd be totally fucked. She loved rock and roll in the first place because it made her feel like she'd live forever as a beautiful creature, complete and fabulous. The plan had been to get a rocker boyfriend who'd immortalize her with a great song like "Brown-Eyed Girl." Once she was described, a part of her would always stay that way—fixed, impossible to dislodge, like one of those croquet balls stuck in the ear. That was what it was about, as far as she was concerned, fixing the moment against loss.

But Eldon never even ventured near the general region of her essence, and she only felt empty and desperate to pour whatever it was those band guys had into herself, but she couldn't get it all in fast enough. There was a leak somewhere.

Eldon watches Connie's shorts ride up as she bends over to pick up a croquet mallet. The sadness of the night sky, which never got very dark, and the immobility of the boy, and the toothpick fragility of Connie's legs—it all sweeps into him. He wants to do something very kind, to take care of some poor thing. He imagines saving the kid in the pool. If he'd only been there earlier, he would have peeled off his shirt, dived in, and fished him out. He wants to be kind to anyone with the exception of Connie. She seems too vapid and messy, too untucked, with her hair flying upward in the wind as she struggles to drag the mallet to the edge of the pool. She's crying, it looks like.

The fact that she might be grieving bothers him, because it hasn't even occurred to him that he might feel grief as well. A fine way to muffle this regret—he knows this instinctively, rather than thinking it—is to suffocate any urge to act kindly toward Connie. He decides to sally back over to his drink.

The ice hasn't yet melted completely.

Across the pool, mallet in hand, Connie cries and doesn't know why. It's for the boy only in the most general way. She just has to see his face, is all; she has to have that. She has to get his secret—he seems so self-contained, such a finished project, and she would like to grab some of that for herself. Maybe it's the Valium but she doesn't feel so great, a little dizzy, but she kneels down anyway and pokes at him with the stick. Up close she can see he's ringed by dead bugs that have been attracted by the light and ended up drowned. A few of them float motionless, then make a last valiant flutter. She jabs the body; first an arm sinks, then a leg. She's sort of pushing him under the surface, but whenever one part of him goes down, another pops up, so that he's never in danger of slipping under completely.

After a couple of tries, she figures the thing to do is to hook the mallet around the side of his body and pull straight back until she manages to maneuver him to the side. She grabs his arm and rolls him over. There he is: his face, his eyes open and looking bad in a way no one really wants described. She crouches and studies him for a few moments. He doesn't look familiar. She's pretty sure she's never seen this guy before. There are millions of identical stars above and thousands of miles of pipes buried below;

this guy could have an affiliation to any one of them. Or to none. She swivels her attention across the pool, where Eldon reclines, swirling a highball.

She could really use a sip of his drink. The inside of her mouth tastes like sushi.

In the water, John floats quietly, sandwiched between the light of the moon and the bulb in the pool below. His hair continues to fan about his face like a living thing. It turns out that Connie was right about him. He even thinks of himself as complete—finished but forgotten, like his life has been written down in a book that's been placed on a shelf in a summer house no one visits much anymore. This particular book is intended as an item of decoration, rather than for reading, anyway. The way it is for him now, bobbing in the pool with open eyes, he has no choice but to stare at the moon, the endlessly described moon, something he once regarded as a dead, dark satellite, but which he now considers a brief, pulsing gem flying through time so quickly that it's almost gone.

It's gone now.

Goodnight

AT THE END of the road is a father, always a father. Snow drives fast, in lipstick, pretending there could be anything at the end of the road—an orphanage, a petting zoo, a houseful of boys, cocktails and tight clothes that expand and float away in the dark. Her left foot hangs out the window, her hair is rough from the wind. Paul is slumped in the passenger seat beside her, quiet and blank, watching one field of wheat bleed into the next. They have made a decision. It was an ordeal, but they did it. They decided to avoid the interstates and take the back roads. In the Midwest, the two-lane highways blend into soil uninterrupted by guardrails or embankments, the shoulders dissolving seamlessly into dirt, stem, the green blanket of agriculture.

"Asleep," she insists.

"Wrong."

"No I'm not. Cozy. Asleep."

Some dark-furred animal, its coat unmarked, is curled

on the shoulder. Miles later there's an orange cat stretched on its side, the tail missing.

"I know," she says.

Snow squints through the windshield. They're going to the house of Paul's father because it's the only place they could think of to go. Where they had been was no longer satisfactory. It was his girlfriend, her best friend, little Juliette, a suicide at twenty-two, and so they had to go. All those verbs: to leave, to travel, to depart, to flee. Snow has refused to let Paul drive; it's her car after all, an aged Rabbit with the "t" cracked off in back. She calls it The Rabbi and steers it over the secondary highways of the Midwest, the Rockies, the far West, pretty much only alert to one thing, the imperative of movement. She keeps her mind on the going and the radio, and plans strategies for the ingestion of coffee. Stopping seems like a very bad idea.

"Can't we go to a diner or something?"

"No." She gives it some thought. "McDonald's drive-through."

"Jesus, Snow." Paul's ears stick out, and she can see the glare of headlights coursing through them. "We're passing all these cool mom-and-pop diners. You're snubbing the real America."

"No. It's weird in those places. I want a milkshake without milk."

"As opposed to real milk in those big, silver dispensers?"

"KKK. Evil cowboys. Fat waitresses."

"Will you talk the fuck in sentences?"

"Okay: Fuck off, Paul."

At a rest stop, they pull over after midnight to sleep for a while. "Wanna go back?" she says. The headlights of passing cars make block shapes that speed across the upholstery. Always, someone is going.

"No." Paul has stretched out the best he can in the back. She won't relinquish the driver's seat. She's not one to let go of something like that. "We decided we would go and we should. We should finish what we start."

"A go-getter."

He was a Boy Scout. She, on the other hand, had always tried her best to weasel her way through life so it didn't hurt so much. This involved a kind of narrowed and selective vision, poor lighting, stopping in the middle and turning back, that sort of thing. And hadn't Juliette stopped in the middle and tried to turn back?

"I want to keep going," Paul says, drowsy, "I want to see my father. Sometimes you want to see your dad, you know?"

"A boy needs his daddy."

"A girl too."

"Please."

Next, he's asleep. Dead to the world, Juliette used to say, the stupid bitch, in a princess nightgown, with sausage curls falling in front of her ears and a charm on her throat that said "#1 Fox." Gusts of traffic noise sift through the window. She pulls the sleeping bag over her shoulders, nostalgic for a clarity to which she may have never been privileged. She looks at the stars clinging to the sky above the windshield, the motherfuckers. The stupid fucking asshole stars.

This particular father lives in a disordered house that bears a peculiar, civet-like scent Snow discerns just for a moment at the time of entrance. The first thing Paul does is to lead her to the refrigerator; it's some symbol of home, apparently, and though it's not very well stocked, he wants them to visit it together. The father emerges from a hallway, hair unkempt, muttering greetings and offering them Schlitz. He's a big, bear-like man with a gut and a beard that both seem strapped on. He supposedly does books for people Paul has never met in a messy room with stacks of magazines piled in front of the windows. For many years he's lived alone. It's apparent to Snow almost immediately that whatever it is they're searching for, this man will be incapable of offering it.

Unfortunately, it's not apparent to the father himself, who begins to question them about the fate of Juliette.

"I was so sorry to hear about . . ." he trails off. Because, Snow realizes, he has forgotten her name. "Your friend," he offers, looking elsewhere. "Paul mentioned it. Sorry, Paul, that there isn't anything to eat. I haven't been getting to the store much."

"I guess we could go out, if you have some money."

"Okay. In a minute. I want to talk to you kids a little bit first."

But then he doesn't have anything to say. Snow watches Paul pace around the kitchen, opening cupboards and examining shelves, as if these small, draftless places have a significance quite apart from their utility. After a long silence, the father speaks.

"You been okay, son?"

"I guess."

"You holding up okay?"

"Yeah."

"Rough time for you . . ."

The way he says it, it's like, "Nice day out there."

Snow thinks she'd like to kill him. She wanders to the sliding glass door and observes the butterfly decals. Outside are trees and grass and maybe a dog. The world is, she knows, irrevocably ugly.

The father and Paul pop open beers, then exchange sentences about the weather, the house, the dog in the yard. They stand in awkward positions for what seems to be an abnormally long period of time. She notes that the two of them treat each other chummily, but with distance, as though they were business associates. Paul talks about a class he took in school, the towns they traveled through, the way Snow refused to let him take the wheel.

"It's a long trip"—the father directs his comment to her—"for someone to drive by themselves."

"I guess."

"A lot of people couldn't do that."

She checks him for signs of condescension. He's slouched against the counter in sweat pants that aren't all that clean. There's something sort of wrong with him. He's like one of those kids who appears halfway through the year in grade school, in the wrong clothes, anticipating another round of rejection. Oddities of stature and of grooming.

"Or we could just get a pizza," he's saying now, "then you kids wouldn't have to go anywhere. I usually send out for pizza. I think the guy even knows me." He looks at her and flashes a pathetic smile she feels obligated to return. Paul is smiling too and for the first time in weeks there's a little color in his cheeks; his eyes are bright and he's taking off his sweater. The heat is returning to his body. He's flushed and in love.

• • •

She stands in the bathroom, pants unbuttoned, giving the medicine cabinet the routine pharmaceutical check. Despite her revulsion at the sight of white tile, warmth rains over her. She's hit pay dirt. Besides the normal run of psychoactive drugs that keep the father halfway functional—Paxil, Wellbutrin, Prozac—Snow discovers a range of pills that enhance the glitter of objects and render any company pleasant company; drugs that deliver a Norman Rockwell mood of Christmas anytime, anyplace, including methadone and a large bottle of Demerol dated six years earlier, probably from when Paul's mother was dying of cancer. She washes a pair down with tap water and slides the bottle into her pocket.

In the kitchen Paul and his father are back to their obsessive discussion of food and meals but they've loosened up somewhat, probably due to the Schlitz.

"Hey, Snow," Paul says, "we've decided we'll do whatever you say."

"You're the boss," the father adds.

"So," Paul chimes in, "what's on the menu?"

They gaze at her, both of them, their eyes open and warm. Paul looks taller and there's something almost flirtatious in his tone; he's happy now. For a moment the weight of grief has floated off him. His father is beside him and so is Snow, his friend, and though the pain of Juliette's exit is in every way intolerable, he is for a moment tolerating it. She looks at him, tolerating it. The traitor.

• • •

They get back in the car. In Snow's stomach a pill breaks open like an egg. Without his father Paul sags somewhat, he loses his glow, and Snow feels all around more comfortable. She has the steering wheel under her palm. The imperative of movement has returned, and again they are going.

"Your father seems kind of . . . I don't know."

"Yeah. He's a lot better than he was. He didn't get out of bed for a year."

"God. What was that about?"

"I don't know. My mom, I guess. But he was kind of like that before."

"Shit," Snow says. "Doesn't it bother you?" Scenery moves past them out the window like something that has been applied to the sky with a spray gun.

"No. Kind of. I mean, he's my dad. He's doing a lot better now." She would never understand what attracted Juliette—so brittle and immersed, so focused on her inner life that it burst out of her like a light, swallowing everything in the vicinity—to Paul, so solid, so like a cow.

In the grocery store they get pasta and vegetables and coffee and eggs. Snow has reached the floating stage in the arc of the drug, which she's taken on an empty stomach. She pushes the cart with one foot and glides on a river of linoleum. Boxes of cereal float past and recede. Candy is bright and individually wrapped. She has reached the staring stage and regards the variety of snack cakes persistently and with something close to awe.

"What is it?" Paul asks.

"Little Debbie," she puts forth, by way of explanation.

All the things Juliette waved good-bye to, all the shiny things in the world.

Back in the car, at the moment of ignition, Snow experiences a twinge of conscience. She shouldn't be driving, perhaps, would be one way of looking at the situation. But that would mean giving up the wheel, maybe even telling Paul she's lit on his dead mother's medication. And once she admits she's not in control, anything could happen. Any of the tragedies could start their parade.

So she drives slowly, and when the dog lopes into the roadway enthusiastically, like an overeager waiter, she heads for him at a crawl, annoyed by Paul's warnings and certain that dog and car will not meet. Slowly she hits the dog, though hard enough to throw him into the gutter, where he lies motionless. Paul maybe has his head in his hands as Snow leaves the car idling in the road and runs to the animal's side. The dog whines softly, his body unnaturally still, as if perhaps there's something wrong with it. The dog's body has the slightly distorted look of a figure drawing by an amateur artist.

"Hey, hey," Snow says, "are you okay?"

His brown eyes are focused and clear but dripping water; they look at Snow with a depth of feeling she's unfamiliar with. He looks at her, quite plainly, with hope.

"Oh man." Paul comes to her side. The way he says it—like it's meant to make Snow feel all sunny about what she's done. He says it again. Then, with sincerity, "Poor guy."

The dog whines some more, then goes slack.

"I can't deal with this," Snow says.

Paul knocks on a door and tells a man, who says that dog has been fucking asking for it and makes some noise about calling the department of waste control. Snow gets back in the car and eats another pill.

"Shall I drive?" Paul asks, when he gets back in. He is kind, Snow thinks, that's what he had for Juliette, though surely she hadn't known what to do with kindness. It would have confused her as something with an arcane set of rules, like cribbage. Still, she held out. She, too, must have looked at him with hope.

When they return to the house they don't mention the dog. Snow and Paul prepare the pasta in the kitchen while the father merrily puts some Bach on the stereo. He calls Paul and Snow into the living room and makes a special event of showing them the record player and a tall stack of vinyl. He calls it a "hi-fi," and obviously expects them to treat it as some rare and impressive hipster artifact. Paul obliges him with a few "wow"s and a "man, is that nice"; Snow would like to hate him for his out-of-date pretension but she's elevated from the pills, and from the Schlitz she's finally accepted. It's the Bach, finally, that brings on the Christmas feeling she's been angling for. The glow of everything is good. She's in the middle of a goddamn Hickory Farms sausage commercial. She forgets the dog. The dog is asleep.

Paul and his father retire to the porch after dinner. The father smokes a pipe, apparently, and likes to release the fumes into the warm night air.

"We have to go back now," Snow says. The ground is a little curved. She's surprised that no one has mentioned she's acting bombed. "I don't think this is good out here. Bad."

"Well," the father says, "I don't want to argue with a lady. But I think it isn't that bad. I think maybe you're just a little bit homesick."

"No," she says. "You don't know that."

"Have you talked to your folks lately?" Paul asks.

"What?"

"Did you tell your folks or your brother about Juliette?"

"Oh my God. Nobody likes me."

"Why do you say that?"

"Snow?" The father is concerned. Like Paul, the father is a kind guy. "Can I get you anything?"

"Not anything. Nothing. I'm just tired."

She finds an empty bedroom and lies down just for a minute. A baby must have slept in the room. There's still pink and blue clown paper on the walls. The Christmas feeling has turned slightly unstable but taking more pills seems like a bad idea. Then she feels warm again, like there's pink light dripping out of her pores. Snow thinks she'd like to be entwined with another creature in a deep way, to feel as she'd felt when she looked into the dog's eyes. To be part of an inseparable pair, incontrovertibly linked in suffering.

When she starts awake what feels like a few minutes later, the night has cooled and the house is quiet. While she's slept, the room has filled up with a choking, palpable darkness packed around her like goose down. She listens to the silence of the house, struggling with the growing conviction that something bad and endless has crept into the room with her. Or it might be inside her, leaking out. It seems like a thing to be fought, so she fights it, her heart pounding in her ears and her palms sweating through the sheets.

She manages to pull herself shivering from the covers. In the kitchen she pulls open the refrigerator and stands in the weak glow of the utility bulb looking at the bare shelves. The tile floor beneath her feet feels cold and disinterested. She leaves the door ajar and travels down another hallway. In a room, she finds the father sitting on a bed in an undershirt, spotlit by a reading lamp. When she looks at him, Snow is bathed with relief. She again feels the pink light dripping from her pores, the warm openness. It's true everything is going to be all right. She knows it with a kind of physical certainty that doesn't require the faculty of reason, the way she might raise an ax and know exactly where it would fall.

The father puts down his Snickers bar and looks at her with a slack face. He stares. Okay, so she's wearing only an undershirt and panties but that doesn't change the fact that she's come seeking brotherhood and connection. She means him no harm.

For a moment, he doesn't speak. He just looks, motionless, his eyes retreating and somehow overly aware of themselves. He glances down briefly as he moves his foot.

"Uh . . ."

"What?"

"Is something wrong?"

The more he looks at her like a trapped animal, the

more Snow becomes convinced that she does, in fact, mean him harm. In fact, she becomes convinced that she means him precisely the kind of harm of which he shows such dread. His hands are tanned with chocolate and his fingers tremble. She squeezes in next to him on the bed, sliding her bottom deliberately across the bedspread. The father grows even paler. She lets her ankle fall across his foot. He holds very still. Her knee brushes lightly against his. Her heart beats with the fury of a predator.

Snow finds she derives a bright, pulsing fullness from the way the father's eyes sink back into his head, as if he's been compacted into some narrow mental hallway. She walks her fingers up his leg and into the crotch of his boxer shorts. What she finds there is yielding but she has an idea she might be able to change that. Sweat glistens between his whiskers and collects on the tip of his nose. She judges him incapable of speech, frozen, though he's breathing in wheezy gasps. She notes that his body emits a brown, civet-like odor as she runs her tongue across his forehead gratefully, her hands on his shoulders, her breasts hanging just below his chin. She feels eminently included in his world, conjoined in misery. For the first time since Juliette's death, she doesn't feel alone.

"How long has it been," she asks, anxious that the moment might slip away, "since you've been with a woman?"

"Wait."

"For what? How long?"

Nothing happens as she kneads his crotch. Obviously. She takes off her top, though, trying to prolong a moment that already seems doomed to end.

When Paul walks into the room, she's standing in front of his father, topless, holding on to his pale, trembling hand. She's watching him sweat.

"What is . . ." Paul says, and then stops. The night is very quiet.

"I'm sorry," his father says, in a high, cramped voice.

Snow turns to look at Paul, standing in the doorway in his faded pajamas, a bad-actor expression of surprise on his face.

Now it is the three of them, all together, all linked.

"Goodnight," Snow says. "Goodnight, goodnight."

A Prodigy of Longing

THE TROUBLE started when my father, Billy, married that bleached and teased powerhouse of hotel management, Skye Near. Skye is a crackpot, that's all there is to it. She believes that back during prehistory Cro-Magnon man was seeded by tall, otherworldly beings with rubbery limbs known as the Nephilim. She thinks these spacemen dropped from the heavens for the express purpose of doing the deed with hairy, slope-browed Cro-Magnon women. Skye herself, with her long legs and freckled skin, considers herself a direct descendant of these star people, who tend to look, as far as I can tell, an awful lot like David Bowie. She got my dad into this stuff too, and before I knew it he was sitting beside her on the couch at weirdo meetings, a cup of tea balanced on his knee, talking with a bunch of batty "scientists" about the possibility of building a rudimentary time warp in the backyard. I sat on the rug, pushing my Hot Wheels from side to side, trying to look feasibly psyched about the prospect of hearing the Gettysburg Address first-hand.

"Wouldn't you like to talk to President Lincoln, son?" a "scientist" asks. "Wouldn't you like to go back in time and sit on the great man's knee?"

I say something like, Oh golly gee, wouldn't that be swell.

Billy is not the sharpest knife in the drawer, but before Skye came along he and I were happy, in our way. I agreed not to use too many polysyllabic words in public; he agreed to put a roof over my head, feed me, and pick me up on time from soccer practice. Sometimes he let me make French toast on Sunday mornings, and in the spring, I'd help him do his taxes. Maybe he wasn't the most attentive dad, but I loved him and appreciated the fact he'd rescued me from my real mom, a dissolute junkie, when I was two years old and he was just nineteen. You know how it is—sometimes we'd throw the ball around; I gave him advice on how to deal with women, including Skye. We had a bond. At least, I thought we had one, until the night I overheard him and Skye talking. I was on the way to the bathroom when I heard Skye's helium voice piercing their door.

"It's not like he'll even *know* about it, Bill."

"But," my dad replied, "he'll probably find out. He can be such an alert little shit."

"You seem to think this is for us," Skye said. "Well, it's not for us. It's for him. My God! By the time he's our age people won't even travel in airplanes anymore! They'll dissolve, and a clone will spring up at their point of destination!"

"The only thing we'll have to worry about then," I heard my dad say, "is blue cheese."

Maybe he didn't actually say "blue cheese." My dad's voice doesn't carry as well as Skye's, but still, I could figure out the gist of their conversation. By that point in my development, I'd long since digested Grimm's fairy tales and figured I'd passed the stage where they might hold much resonance for me. But when I heard my father and Skye murmuring that night, I knew how Hansel and Gretel felt when they discovered their father conspiring with their stepmother to abandon them in the forest. Earlier in the evening I'd asked Skye to reach me down a glass from the cupboard. She'd complied with maternal sweetness. Now she was telling my dad that I didn't need my body, that my body was extraneous.

"C'mon, Bill. It'll be okay. Have a little faith in the future!"

I could tell she was getting to him; she was probably peeling down to her Victoria's Secret thong, and after a little more pleading I heard him reluctantly agree to her scheme: I would be a Head Only, while he and Skye were contracted for the deluxe, more expensive Full Body. What this meant was that as soon as I was pronounced legally dead, a representative from Lactor Corp., a nonprofit cryonics firm, would rush my tender, iced carcass to their state-of-the-art facilities, where a heavy-thewed technician would sever my neck from my shoulders with a surgical saw. My body would be unceremoniously cremated; my head would be pumped full of glycerol, wrapped in plastic, and submerged in a vat full of liquid nitrogen, where it would wait, a disgusting brain Popsicle, to be perhaps thawed at some point in the future when technology had advanced to the point where I could be repaired, or recured, or oh, by the way, they'd be able to clone me a whole new body by then.

Skye and my dad, on the other hand, were to be frozen whole, intact, with every organ and scar they'd waltzed through life with. Maybe they'd be thawed out for centuries, zooming around with personal jet packs, laughing and tossing a tablecloth over the freezer where I lay, spreading a feast of roasted squab inches from my severed head. They'd be partying for centuries before anyone even figured out how to fix me.

Skye and Billy wouldn't need new bodies. They'd already have bodies. It didn't seem fair. I mean, I knew they were fucking crazy but I didn't want to get left behind.

Compounding the problem was the boy next door, who worked on his motorcycle in the autumn evenings when the oak tree in the yard was lit up in the fading light. The boy next door was beautiful and wild. I spent a lot of time outside, lobbing a football up in the air, just to be near him. I just wanted to watch him, his jaw slack with concentration, as he turned and ratcheted things on his machine. He was maybe nineteen, slim and pale (a potential son of the Nephilim), with faraway hazel eyes staring out of his wonderful, never-to-be-removed head. Skye referred to him as "that cute little mortal boy," due to the fact that he (like nearly everyone we knew) had not contracted with Lactor to be cryogenically suspended at the death moment. As far as we knew, the mortal boy was scheduled to die at his death moment.

I guess he noticed me hanging around outside because after a few months of this he began to give me some half waves now and then, the kind you can disguise as a face scratch if the other person doesn't wave back. But usually he ignored me in favor of some mechanical task. The boy was slight but he had a pretty good mustache going that gave him a vital, manly quality. Beneath the mustache his face was sorrowful, like maybe his vitality included a heightened sensitivity to pain.

"Just tell that mortal boy hello," Skye said, watering her pansies with a little green can. He was the only person Skye referred to as mortal, as though there were something especially fleshy, perishable, and earthbound about him. "Just look him in the eye and smile. For God's sake, learn to mix."

I threw the ball up in the air and told Skye I had no idea what she was talking about. But the truth was I thought I could bear the indignity of being a Head Only if the boy were to be decapitated and frozen beside me. We could hang, suspended, staring for centuries into each other's frozen, plastic-wrapped eyes, and neither of us would notice that the other was incomplete. If, by the time they defrosted us, it was really possible to use nanotechnology to repair our bodies on a cell-by-cell basis, then I didn't see why they couldn't make the mortal boy love me, despite the fact that he barely knew I existed and probably had a girlfriend.

Okay, it was a stupid idea. But desire is stupid. It makes people do idiotic things. I think it made my dad marry Skye.

• • •

A week or two after I overheard my dad and Skye talking about cutting off my head, Skye got up earlier than usual and caught me reading at the kitchen table. I tried to hide the book behind the Cheerios box but she was too fast for me.

"What's that, Slugger?" Slugger is my dad's nickname for me. Skye's always trying to ingratiate herself with Billy, even when he's not around. "Is that a school book?"

"Yeah, Skye. It's for school. It's for social studies."

I was reading *Either/Or*, the section about the unhappiest man. In particular, I was interested in Kierkegaard's discussion of the misery inherent in hope—the desperation of one who perpetually longs for an imagined future, or an idealized past—an unhappiness so profoundly alienating one may even be divided from the knowledge that one is suffering from it. I thought maybe this was Skye's big problem.

She tipped the book and looked at the cover. "Søren Kierkegaard? Wait, I've heard of him! He's a painter, right?" Skye was juicing an orange in lavender sweats and pink running shoes, her yellow hair scratching around in a ponytail, steeling herself for her grueling two-mile jog around the lake. Skye looked like a stupid little bunny in her sweat suit but I knew she was involved in layers of deception and calculation that would dazzle a professor of mathematics. Her ruthlessness in manipulating the staff at the Comfort Inn was legendary, and I'd learned to tread carefully when dealing with her seemingly inane comments. There had already been a series of *discussions* with Billy about my behavior, vocabulary, and general apprehension of things that turn, fasten, or hinge, wherein Billy felt compelled to escort me outside, behind the garage, where we had most of our man-to-mans:

"Would you mind dumbing it down a little? Can't you just play with your Hot Wheels in front of her or something?"

"No one my age plays with Hot Wheels."

"She doesn't know that."

It was typical during these discussions to find Billy's hair out of whack and his armpits soaked. I guess he was afraid Skye was going to get freaked out by my general acumen and run off, though it seemed clear to everyone else that she'd settled in for the duration. But Billy was anxious, and for his sake, I tried my best to play dumb. This took a fair amount of vigilance, and when I learned about the whole cryonics conspiracy I sort of lost my motivation and started bringing home books I shouldn't have. I also began to put in a lot of hours flopped out on my bed, staring at that stupid Super Mario poster my dad put up over my dresser to make the room look more "normal." It depicted Mario, a small, two-dimensional Italian man, leaping to rescue a small blond princess from a booby-trapped tower. The princess sort of looked like Skye, which just depressed me more.

"Wouldn't it be easier," Skye remarked, "to get a spaceman to come down and rescue her from above? Then that little guy could go home and have a sandwich."

I said something like Gee, Skye, that is *such* a great idea.

Anyway, Skye obviously mentioned the Kierkegaard to my dad because not long after he got home from work he came outside and glowered at me. I was pretending to lob a football up against the oak tree for the pure satisfaction of it, but I was really waiting to see if the mortal boy would come out of his house.

Dad slipped in and slapped my butt, where I'd secreted the paperback.

"What's that, Slugger?"

"Hey, Dad. That would be a book."

He slid the book out of my pocket and flipped through the pages, putting on an engrossed expression like he was really *absorbing* it. Like I said, Billy was a nice guy who did his best to be a good dad, but he only had an associate's degree in computer programming and usually floundered if he found himself in the vertiginous realms of abstraction, metaphor, and lateral thinking.

"I'm disappointed in you." He shook his head. "This is college stuff."

"Lots of guys are reading it around school, Dad."

In truth, Billy had restricted my library card to the juvenile section. I'd taken to hanging around by the counter, trying to get kids with unrestricted cards to check out the *Symposium* for me.

"Hey, kid, if it was just me, you could do whatever you wanted"—Billy had slipped into his I Am Such a Nice Father mode—"but what do you think Skye makes of all this? Can't you just act your age? I don't want her thinking you're some kind of freak." I watched him slide my Kierkegaard into his briefcase. "C'mon. Let's play some ball. Let's forget about this book stuff and throw the ball around."

We went around to the backyard where there was more room. I tried to humor him for a while, catching the football and throwing it back as hard as I could.

• • •

I was seized, around this time, by an intense fear of death. All the textures of my little life seemed elegiac—the drift of autumn leaves across a lawn, the sound of Billy's car pulling out of the driveway, the shadow of the boy moving behind the curtains next door. In school I began to sit in the back of the room. I grew quiet in the cafeteria while the girls talked about what color T-shirts were the coolest and which movie stars they were going to have sex with when they were a couple of years older. Late afternoons were the worst. The setting sun made me feel like I was going to die. I know this is strange for an eleven-year-old. We always just said I was a prodigy, if we said anything at all, but that word could hardly contain the scope and sadness with which I understood the world to be perishing, its creatures fading from minute to minute, crossing from the green streets of my neighborhood into the mulch of nothingness. By then I'd noticed that I was starting to believe some of that crackpot stuff—the fireballs, the nanotechnology, the death and resurrection. I was afraid that one day I was going to fall off my bike, bounce across the asphalt, and drop into a heavy sleep. By the time they revived me, all the things I loved would have disappeared. I might even be an adult.

One evening in the midst of this despair, I tossed my football up in the air once, twice, and on the third time watched it tumble, fall, and bounce across the yard and roll to a stop next to the mortal boy's sneakers. The boy knelt in front of his motorcycle in a torn jacket, his corn-colored hair sticking up every which way. He scooped up the ball, turned it over, then set it down on the driveway. For about five minutes, I waited for him to toss it back.

He was, I thought, working on his bike, but when I finally got up the nerve to walk across the little berm separating his property from ours, I saw he was bent over a small plastic bag containing dried plant parts that *had* to be marijuana. He didn't bother to look at me as he touched a match to what I took to be a joint. This was grown-up stuff, the big leagues. He put it to his lips, sucked, then handed it to me.

"I can't smoke that."

"Why not?"

"I'm too young."

"Fuck that."

I inhaled a little bit, like they do in the movies. Then I coughed for like a half hour.

"That's okay," he said, and passed me the joint again. We stayed there for a while, I on my feet and he squatting on the driveway, staring into the chrome curves of his motorcycle.

"Nice," I said, and then a little while later: "Bike."

It was evening. The sky was pink, then lavender, then dark blue above and spotted with planets full of Nephilim gazing down at us through telescopes. They were our makers, and we were their science project. I reached over and stroked his arm. His skin felt like a chamois cloth. I knew I wasn't supposed to want this, and so only wanted it more.

Skye pulled into the driveway and honked. I told the mortal boy I had to go home.

"Fuck," he said. He stuck out his foot and kicked over his motorcycle.

• • •

After that, I had the opportunity to spend a fair amount of time with the boy next door. Billy and Skye were becoming even more involved with their weirdo friends and were too busy to pay much attention to me. Some days I'd come in from school and Skye would be home early, bustling around the kitchen, cutting up cheese and fruit. Later, a bunch of people would come over for a meeting. A few of the ladies pinched my cheek; some rough-and-tumble guy who probably thought kids just *loved* him would pick me up and swing me around by my waist until I felt sick. Billy would instruct me to go play in the yard, and then the whole bunch would retreat into the family room and shut the door.

I'd say Golly, Dad, I'll go play hopscotch in traffic.

After these meetings, the two of them were vacant and distracted. Skye hummed merrily—that was always bad news—while my dad grabbed a beer out of the fridge and went into the living room where he'd turn on the radio, fire up the TV, and spread a newspaper across his lap. Sometimes I'd run around making motorcar noises just to help raise the general level of distraction. I mean, what were they shutting out? What crackpot theory of microwave brain control were they trying to outwit?

At least I had plenty of leisure time to tag along with the mortal boy (aka Kelly Sheridan), who usually didn't voice any objections to my presence. It was getting colder so I visited him now in his garage, where he endlessly tuned and retuned his bike, a BMW R75/5, with a stainless steel "toaster" gas tank, that didn't seem to actually run. I'd hold his tools and ask him how things worked, more to hear the rumble of his voice than for the information per se. He didn't talk much otherwise, and it took me a few weeks to piece together a little biography for him: he lived with his dad, his mother was already dead, he was enrolled in junior college. His father wanted him to get a job but he called that notion bullshit. He was waiting, he said. He was making preparations.

Though his slash five wasn't running, he still liked, as he put it, to "roam," and I began to tag along after him on search-and-destroy missions through the neighborhood. Up the street was a condemned hotel formerly known as The Flamingo. The Flamingo seemed like it had once been grand in a middle-class way, but by the time we got there it was a pink husk. Most of the windows were broken but some furniture remained: dressers, suspiciously stained mattresses, tasseled lampshades. The rooms on the upper levels were infested by pigeons and the mortal boy liked to rush into a room waving his arms so that the whole flock took flight at once, whirling through the window like they'd been sucked out by an exhaust fan. If we entered a room quietly they'd just sit on the excrement-frosted furniture, bobbing their heads.

Kelly called it the Birdhouse, as in "Let's go to the Birdhouse," and then he wouldn't say anything for the next half hour. We'd go there and he'd scare the pigeons, then spray paint cryptic slogans on the walls—*Soylent Green Es Personas*—and look at me, and smile, or else not smile.

I tried to act all grown-up around him and said stuff like, "Hey, man, what's the score?" Or, "My stepmom, that bitch, she's on my back twenty-four seven," but he rarely answered. His silence was evocative, rather than vapid, and it made me feel that he might possess something crucial that I, perhaps, lacked. We were sitting on the edge of a busted-out third-story window trying to spear pigeons with shards of mirror when I finally spat it out.

"Hey man. Dude. Do you, like, have a girlfriend?"

"You're just a kid," he said. He aimed a slice of mirror at a senile-looking bird below.

"Okay," I allowed. All around, our neighborhood chugged through its pathetic existence—the roofs were spread out in rows, surrounded by skirts of lawn. Every here and there a dog barked rhythmically in a yard, like a little engine powering the house. "Do all boys," I finally asked, "fall in love with girls?"

The mortal boy didn't say anything for a long time. Then, speaking as though he were plucking words from an infinite number of mistakes, bad choices, and violations of etiquette, he finally said, "I don't want to say anything because I don't know what to say." Then he took the whole mirror, frame and all, and pitched it out the window.

As we were walking home, a group of teenagers pulled up beside us in a van. They were smoking cigarettes and the girls wore backpacks. Without a word, Kelly climbed in the back and was whisked away.

I guess I'd scratched myself up pretty well that afternoon, actually, since Skye sort of freaked out when she saw a streak of blood on the back of my shirt. I think it happened while I was climbing through a broken window, but I told her I had no idea how it happened. I knew I'd get in trouble if I admitted to visiting the Birdhouse. Anyway, I didn't feel like explaining. I was despondent, not only about the mortal boy abandoning me, but about all of it: the nearness of death, the betrayal of my parents, the sense of longing I disguised as hope that divided me from the simple, childhood pleasures that should have been mine. There is an unhappiness, Kierkegaard says, that has to do with insatiable hope, a hunger that once fulfilled converts itself into a refreshed yearning for something else. For some time I'd judged myself too young to suffer from such a rarefied level of disappointment, but I'd begun to toy with the possibility that maybe I really *wasn't* too young. I'd read that most prodigies were good at a single thing while the rest of their development stayed at normal levels. Maybe that was what I was: a prodigy of longing.

Musing on this, it didn't take a whole lot of effort to sit still as Skye got out the alcohol and cotton balls and set to work on my back.

"This is," she informed me, "an absolutely clean wound. Did you, what, get winged by a knife?"

I told her I had no idea. She went to the laundry room and came back with a big first-aid kit. To my surprise, she began dressing the wound like an expert. I slumped listlessly, watching cartoons, trying to laugh at appropriate moments.

"So, Slugger . . . What'd you get into anyway?"

"I don't know. Nothing."

"Do you remember coming home from school?" She was using this artfully casual tone.

"Duh."

"Duh. Right. But what, after that—?" She let this sink in. On television, teenagers with bulging muscles flew through the air. "Blank spots, hallucinations? Playing with your little friend? What?"

"But Skye," I said, all innocence, "I came directly home from school."

She moved in front of me and tilted my chin up to get a better view of my eyes. I think it's safe to say she was trembling, ever so slightly. "William," she said, "I want you to look at the clock and tell me what time it is."

I looked at the clock. I gasped. It was already six!

"William," she was absolutely glowing, "tell me again how you got this cut."

"Mom," I said, "I swear I don't know."

"Oh my God!" Skye gathered me in her arms. "My poor baby. My poor, poor baby boy."

Skye was convinced I'd been abducted by aliens, Small Grays, who had made the slit in my back to obtain genetic information and perhaps harvest blood products. I lay in bed, covered by quilts, as Skye's crackpot friends shuffled in to prod, question, and examine me.

"He was acting all blank," she whispered. "He was sitting there watching cartoons and—my God!—*laughing*, while I field-dressed his wound!"

Several crackpots agreed that this was very strange indeed. Meanwhile, Skye's astrologer, Renée, sat by the bed and massaged my temples with oil. Renée had yellow teeth and always looked really tired—"partied out," my dad said—but I liked her because sometimes she gave me drags off her cigarettes.

"You just relax, kiddo," she said. "Let any old thought drift through your brain that wants to get in there."

I relaxed and thought of the mortal boy climbing into the back of the van with his friends.

"I see the stumpy kind," Renée began, her voice raspy, closing her eyes and rocking from side to side, griping my temples—this Vulcan mind-meld stunt had obviously entered the culture through old *Star Trek* episodes. "I am seeing them in a silver pod. Oh man. Membranes. One is floating. A human being on a table. Light, light. Okay, I am seeing them doing some bad shit to a little boy—oh man!" She tore her hands off my temples—"The probe! I am seeing the probe!"

Renée pulled out a pack of cigarettes. "Fucking A. We gotta purify him."

The women retreated to the hallway to confer with the other crackpots about my rape by Small Grays—a drone species at war with our sensitive, watchful benefactors, the Nephilim. Skye lit up one of Renée's cigarettes and looked at our furniture with bright, excited eyes.

I, meanwhile, played my part to the hilt, staring ahead glassily or tossing about, as if with fever. When Skye returned, I began to mumble in terror, "The probe, the probe."

Skye stroked my hair. One of the crackpots laid a cold compress across my forehead. Skye began to hum softly. It wasn't the merry humming she used to fool the alien microwaves, but a soft, tender melody that brought back the feeling of falling asleep on the lawn after swimming on a hot day.

I had to remind myself that this was the woman who had engineered my postmortem decapitation.

When my dad got home, I was lying naked beneath a sheath of steaming towels with an ice pack on my forehead. In addition to Skye and Renée, about a half dozen other oddballs were wandering around our house, tapping information into laptops, recording my vital signs, whispering into the telephone. I was sweating beneath the towels, my hair plastered flat, occasionally mumbling evocative words like "pellicle," "immiscible," and "ischemia" while a guy hovered over me with one of those really small tape recorders. Billy walked into my room, took one look at the mayhem, and hit the roof.

"Out," he said, through clenched teeth. The fact that he was *not* yelling was particularly scary. "Everyone. Now. Outside."

The room cleared, except for Skye. "It's not his fault," she said. "We think it was the little ETs."

"Out," he said, his face red. What a tough guy. I, myself, was petrified. I knew I wasn't too old to spank.

But when the room emptied, the door closed, and it was just the two of us, he turned his bloodshot eyes on me and I could tell that his anger had sagged, to be replaced by a weary sadness I found far more threatening.

He dropped into the chair beside my bed. "You know you shouldn't tease her. It's too easy." He took off his jacket. One of his pens had leaked a big Rorschach onto his shirt. As usual when dealing with me, Billy seemed exhausted. "You need to realize you're not like other people. That's part of the problem. You know it, and Skye knows it. She's looking for an explanation. . . ."

"Skye's a nut."

"I don't want to hear you talk about your stepmom like that. Not ever. She's not a nut. She's spiritual. I don't want your smart mouth scaring her off, understand?"

"Yes, Dad."

"Fuck. I wish you'd call me Billy sometimes." He began to peel soggy towels off my chest. "This is disgusting."

"You know," I began, "I heard what you guys said about freezing my head." At this point, I figured it was impossible to disappoint him anymore. "It doesn't seem fair."

"Jesus, Slugger, by the time you're my age, they'll have death cured."

"What if I died tomorrow?"

I guess I was crying a little because that always pisses Billy off. "Don't be such a pussy," he said. "Most people don't even get to be frozen. Be grateful you get a second chance."

He threw the last of the towels onto the carpet. I'd been steaming for over an hour and my skin was puckered and red. I knew I shouldn't have said what I did then, but I couldn't help it. I just felt like my life was always going to contain this huge omission, that I was always going to be partial if something wasn't done.

"Can I bring a friend? Billy? Can we at least have Kelly Sheridan go Head Only too?"

"Christ. That creep next door?" He shambled out of the room muttering under his breath like I wasn't even worth answering directly.

After he left, Skye came in and wiped the snot off my face with a warm washcloth.

Skye refused to revise her opinion that I'd been abducted by aliens, despite my father's insistence that it was a hoax, I was a bad seed, and I should be handled with extreme skepticism or else ignored as much as possible. I, in turn, had revised my judgment of Skye from Nutcase to Lucid Nutcase. To tell the truth, I was sort of beginning to like her. I began to understand how it must have been difficult for her to find herself living with a guy like me. I'm pretty sure she was in love with me, in that way grown-up ladies fall in love with little boys. I mean, even before the abduction it was clear a lot of the time that she was as interested in me as she was in my dad—buying me Superman sheets, heating up mini pizzas, laughing at my knock-knock jokes. Sometimes I even theorized that it was her bewilderment at finding herself in love with such an odd, secretive creature that got her involved with the UFO community in the first place. Because if she loved a freak like me, what did that mean about her? It could only mean she'd been tampered with by aliens. That was how her brain worked.

But after the abduction, it was like I'd crossed some line and joined Skye's secret club. She began to buy me stickers of bug-eyed aliens and encouraged me to put them on my notebooks.

"Recognize this guy?" she asked, slapping a cool, holographic sticker of an elongated smiley face on my bicycle fender.

I'd just sort of look at her and laugh. I didn't really know what to say. I was going through some changes then myself. Maybe I was beginning to get hormones; I'm not sure. I do know that I began to find myself so disoriented at the moment of waking—so without a sense of place or destination—that I began to wonder if maybe Skye wasn't on to something. At times I thought I was back with my junkie mom, in that cold apartment, with *Houses of the Holy* playing in the next room. Or I thought I'd slipped back to the period when Billy and I lived in an uneasy truce, before the arrival of Skye, in a quiet bedroom lit by an orange night-light. Or, sometimes, there was something else: a silver tube filled with ashen beings, their eyes coated by a greenish pellicle, moving through an immiscible atmosphere of oil and water. A band is around my biceps and my fingers tingle with ischemia. I'm not sure what did happen that afternoon. Maybe I did lose a few hours. Maybe I blanked because of the probe. I don't know. What I do know is that in those slim crescents between sleep and waking, right before I was flooded with doubt, I was happy. In the uncertainty of where the hell I was, I finally possessed a certainty of who I am.

It was a weird moment, but I was living right in the middle of it.

A crew of workmen appeared and began to install green vinyl siding around the mortal boy's house. They started at the bottom and worked their way up, building a progressively thicker shell of pea-colored plastic. There was something insect-like about the whole venture; the house itself came to resemble a giant cocoon. Kelly's dad came over one Sunday and gave Billy a rundown on the virtues of siding, as though everyone on earth didn't already know it never needed to be painted. I sat in the corner listening, wearing down my crayons.

I hadn't seen Kelly for a couple of months, since the day he'd jumped in the van, but once the siding was up I began to hear occasional rumblings from his garage. Sometimes I noticed a trail of exhaust creeping out from under the door. At around the same time, the phenomenon started in my hands. At night I'd hold them under the covers and watch them emit a faint greenish glow. I had several theories about this. One: I'd lost my marbles. Two: I was just trying to be like Skye, who was being so solicitous toward me I sometimes thought I might swoon. Every day she let me have one of those TV dinners with the soupy brownies at the top. Every day she told me if I wanted to, I should go ahead and eat the brownie first.

Then there was theory three: influence from the air.

Before, Skye usually wore business suits with padded shoulders, nylons, and a ton of jewelry. She had a lot of suits in all one color with contrasting trim—a dark green gabardine with yellow piping—that made her look really stupid. But after the abduction, Skye began favoring print dresses with wide, puffy skirts. She sometimes wore those with aprons when she worked in the kitchen, and she'd taken to doing her hair differently too. It was smaller, with gray coming in at the temples, and it looked sort of molded or lacquered. When she went out sometimes she'd wear a little pillbox hat and gloves.

I quite admired her new look and her renewed interest in home economics. She'd changed her schedule so she got off before Billy, and in the afternoons we'd go to the park and play. Skye really liked flying kites, even in winter, and afterward she'd buy me ice cream or French fries. Flying kites with Skye was really fun; she'd reach her arms around me and show me how to make them go way up, and I'd pretend like she was teaching me. She'd whisper fairy tales about the Nephilim—how they watched and loved us and tried to help us through the hard parts of our lives; how they ate mint wafers the size of Frisbees for breakfast, lunch, and dinner. I just liked being near her and taking whiffs of her grape-scented hair spray. She was so nice to me that I stopped caring that she was insane. Some days, I may have even stopped noticing.

Skye and I were in the kitchen having cookies and milk on the first really warm day of spring when the mortal boy finally emerged from his garage. We had a lot of flies that spring and Skye had hung plastic bags full of water in front of the windows because she'd read in some women's magazine that refracted light freaked flies out. They'd look at it with their eighteen eyes, and all they'd want was to fly the hell elsewhere. Skye was looking especially weird, with bubbles of light swinging across her face, when we heard the knock on the door.

She peeked through the window. "It's your little friend."

"Tell him I'm not here."

"For Pete's sake, William." She had begun to use this maternal, June Cleaver tone around me. "Scoot out there and say hello to that poor boy. Don't be such a bookworm."

She flung open the door. Kelly stood on the stoop, his corn-colored hair sticking up on one side of his head, a motorcycle helmet cradled in his arms.

"Can he come out?" He nodded in my direction. There was a touch of John Wayne in the way he addressed Skye—earnest and courtly.

"He'd love to."

The screen door thudded shut behind me. The next thing I knew I was standing close enough to Kelly to mull over his oily, dirty-hair smell. There was a hole in the toe of his sneaker. Another motorcycle helmet sat on the ground beside his feet. Behind me, Skye was peeking out through the curtains. I guess I was her science project now.

For a while Kelly just stood there, studying the shiny surface of his helmet. Then, with extreme effort, as though every word released another pound of air pressure from an absolutely irreplaceable tire, he said: "I'm going now, if you want to come with."

"You haven't talked to me in two months."

He kicked at the mud. "I was making preparations."

"Where are you going?"

"Just going. Hit the road. It'll be cool." He looked me in the eye. "We'll say you're my little brother."

I checked my hands. In the sunlight you couldn't see the glow, but I could feel it. This might sound stuck-up, but for once I knew I had a light belonging only to me. Whatever exotic substance the mortal boy had once seemed made of, he didn't seem to be made of it anymore. Or I'd come into possession of an exotic substance myself.

"I have to ask my stepmom," I said.

Kelly looked me in the face. "Shit," he said, and walked halfway across the lawn to his house. Then he stopped and turned back to me.

"Shit," he said again, sticking out his hip and shaking his head like he was John Wayne and he'd lost a herd of cows.

I mean, what was I supposed to do? After all, I am just a little kid.

The mortal boy shuffled into his garage, swung a leg over his bike, got it started—truly a miracle—and rolled down the driveway, out of my neighborhood and out of my life.

After he was gone it only seemed natural that I'd go too, with Skye, when she finally decided to leave my dad and move to New Mexico. Alien abductions and cattle mutilations were commonplace there, she said. We'd be closer to the source.

My dad was against my going, but I had almost nothing left in common with him. Since the incident, Skye had become the undisputed queen of the UFO weirdos. She liked to sit on the couch with me nestled at her side, answering questions about the true nature of the Alien Planet Surface as if she'd recently vacationed there. My dad would lean against the doorway, looking at us like we were a couple of Head Onlys and he was the sole Full Body in the whole neighborhood. I guess I wanted to go with Skye. She was trying to act like a good mom, even if sometimes I thought she was faking it.

Now we live in a subdivision outside Albuquerque. I really like it here. Kierkegaard talked about living in a castle on a peak and only darting down to the world of reality occasionally to "seize his prey." He thought a guy ought to stand apart so he could pick over his experiences from a safe place. It's been kind of like that for me since we've been in New Mexico. The desert seems empty at first but it holds amazing possibilities—living at its edge is like living at the edge of an ocean. It spits things up: odors, old tires, lights, whatever. At night if I aim the radio in its direction I can pick up weird shows about fornication and the blood of Jesus, or dramas about sea captains roaming the deck with a hatchet and spyglass. If there's bad weather, the signals bleed together so it's sort of like Jesus is limping the deck with a hatchet and a spyglass. And sometimes, I hear something else—something swarming and warm, the call of my own. I'm able to hear it now that I've finally figured out that human relationships are like the bags of water Skye hangs in the windows to repel flies. My theory is this: if we get too close to people on earth, it might distract us from the things in the air. Something is going to save me, I know that with certainty now. Someone is going to fly down and take care of me in a way that really matters.

My favorite thing to do is to sneak outside after Skye has fallen asleep and ride my bike over a dirt track into the desert. It's beautiful there, under the ceiling of stars. I usually take my gloves off then. The glow spreads to my elbows now and once a little flame of it forked all the way up to my collarbone. I know I belong somewhere else, in a place where there are others like me. It won't be like it is down here. Everyone will be made of one thing, and love will be safe.